The Million-in-One Man

The extermination engineers had erected barriers between the Red and the Green zones. In the Green, the men had done their work well—no useless insects survived. But they still had to clear the way in the Red zone, to destroy insect life there—a lower form of life which was presenting a threat to mankind.

The Indian waited at the barrier to be let into the Green zone; he simulated the servility which would identify him as a primitive from the deep Brazilian interior—from the Red zone.

At the barrier he was almost overcome with the repellants sprayed at him. But the brilliant facets of his eyes, the tiny scales of his skin were not detected. The weave of furry separate cells did not become unravelled.

The million-in-one man penetrated the uninfested Green.

Tor Books by Frank Herbert

THE
GREEN BRAIN

FRANK HERBERT

A TOM DOHERTY ASSOCIATES BOOK
NEW YORK

This is a work of fiction. All the characters and events portrayed in this book are either products of the author's imagination or are used fictitiously.

THE GREEN BRAIN

Part of this novel has appeared in *Amazing stories* as a novelette entitled *Greenslaves* and is copyright © 1965 by Ziff-Davis Publications, Inc.

A Tor Book
Published by Tom Doherty Associates, LLC
175 Fifth Avenue
New York, NY 10010

www.tor.com

Tor® is a registered trademark of Tom Doherty Associates, LLC.

ISBN: 0-765-34250-2

First Tor edition: September 2002

Printed in the United States of America

0 9 8 7 6 5 4 3 2 1

1

He looked pretty much like the bastard offspring of a Guarani Indio and some backwoods farmer's daughter, some *sertanista* who'd tried to forget her enslavement to the *encomendero* system by "eating the iron"—which is what they call lovemaking through the grill of a consel gate.

The type-look was almost perfect except when he forgot himself while passing through one of the deeper jungle glades.

His skin tended to shade down to green then, fading him into the background of leaves and vines, giving a ghostly disembodiment to the mud-gray shirt and ragged trousers, the inevitable frayed straw hat and rawhide sandals soled with pieces cut from worn tires.

Such lapses grew less and less frequent the farther he emerged from the Parana headwaters, the *sertao* hinterland of Goyaz where men with his bang-cut black hair and glittering dark eyes were common.

By the time he reached *bandeirantes* country, he had

achieved almost perfect control over the chameleon effect.

Now, he was out of the wilder jungle growth and into the brown dirt tracks that separated the parceled farms of the resettlement plan. In his own way, he knew he was approaching one of the bandeirante checkpoints, and with an almost human gesture he fingered the *cedula de graicias al sacar*, the certificate of white blood, tucked safely beneath his shirt. Now and again, when humans were not near, he practiced aloud the name that had been chosen for him—"Antonio Raposo Tavares."

The sound emerged a bit strident, harsh on the edges, but he knew it would pass. It already had. Goyaz Indios were notorious for the strange inflections of their speech. The farm folk who'd given him a roof and food the previous night had said as much.

When their questions had become pressing, he'd squatted on their doorstep and played his flute, the *qena* of the Andes Indian, which he carried in a leather purse hung from his shoulder. The gesture of the flute was a symbol of the region. When a Guarani put flute to nose and began playing, that said words were ended.

The farm folk had shrugged and retired.

His trudging progress, the difficult and carefully mastered articulation of legs, had brought him now into an area of many humans. He could see red-brown rooftops ahead and the white crystal shimmering of a bandeirante tower with its aircars alighting and departing. The scene held an odd hive-look.

Momentarily, he found himself overcome by the touch of instincts that he knew he must master. These instincts could make him fail the ordeal to come. He stepped off the dirt track, out of the path of passing humans, and went through the regimen that united his mental identity. The resultant thought penetrated to the smallest and most remote units of his person: *We are greenslaves subservient to the greater whole.*

He resumed his way toward the bandeirante checkpoint. The unifying thought lent him an air of servility that was like a shield against the stares of humans trudging past all around. His kind knew many human mannerisms. They had learned early that servility was a form of concealment.

Presently, the dirt track gave way to a two-lane paved market road with footpaths in the ditches on both sides. This, in turn, curved alongside a four-deck commercial transport highway where even the footpaths were paved. Now there were groundcars and aircars in greater numbers, and the flow of foot traffic increased.

Thus far he'd attracted no dangerous attention. The occasional snickering side-glance from natives of the area could be safely ignored. He watched for probing stares. These could hold peril, but he detected none.

Servility shielded him.

The sun stood well along toward mid-morning and the day's heat had begun to press down on the earth, raising a moist hothouse stink from the dirt beside the pathway, mingling it with the perspiration odors of humanity around him. There was a sourness to the smell that made every part of him long for the sweetly familiar odors of the hinterland. And the lowland smells carried another harmonic that filled him with an inaudible humming of unease. Here were greater and greater concentrations of insect poisons.

Humans were all around him now, close and pressing, moving slower and slower as they approached the checkpoint bottleneck.

The forward motion stopped.

Progress resolved itself into shuffle and stop, shuffle and stop. . . .

Here was the critical test and no avoiding it. He waited with something akin to an Indian's stoic patience. His breathing had grown deeper to compensate for the heat. He adjusted it to match that of the humans around him, suffering the temperature rise for the sake of blending into his surroundings. Andes Indians didn't breathe deeply here in the lowlands.

Shuffle and stop.

Shuffle and stop.

Now he could see the checkpoint.

Fastidious bandeirantes in sealed white cloaks with plastic helmets, gloves and boots stood in a double row within a shaded brick corridor leading into the town. He could see sunlight hot on the street beyond the corridor, people hurrying away there after passing this gantlet.

The sight of that free area beyond the corridor sent an ache of longing through all the parts of him. The suppression warning flashed out instantly on the heels of that instinctive reaching-emotion.

No distraction could be permitted here. Every element of him had to be alert to withstand the pain.

Shuffle and . . . he was into the hands of the first bandeirante, a hulking blond fellow with pink skin and blue eyes.

"Step along now! Lively now!" the fellow said.

A gloved hand propelled him toward two bandeirantes standing on the right side of the line.

"Name?" *That was a voice behind him.*

"Antonio Raposo Tavares," he rasped.

"District?"

"Goyaz."

"Give that one an extra treatment," the blond giant

called. "He's from the upcountry for certain."

The two waiting bandeirantes had him now, one jamming a breather mask over his face, the other dropping a plastic bag over him. A tube trailed from the bag and out toward the sound of machinery somewhere in the street beyond the corridor.

"Double shot!" one of the bandeirantes called.

Fuming blue gas puffed out the bag around him, and he inhaled a sharp, gasping breath through the mask, astonished at that unanimous demand for poison-free air.

Agony!

The gas drove through every multiple linkage of his being with needles of pain.

We must not weaken, he thought. *Hold fast.*

But it was a deadly pain, killing. Linkages began to weaken.

"Okay on this one," the bag handler called.

The bag was slipped off, breather mask pulled away. Hands propelled him down the corridor toward the sunlight.

"Lively now! Don't hold up the line."

The stink of the poison gas lay all around him. It was a new one—a dissembler. They hadn't prepared him for this poison. He'd been ready for the radiations and the sonics and the old chemicals . . . but not for this.

Sunlight beat down on him as he emerged from the corridor into a street. He veered left through a passage lined by fruit stalls, merchants bartering with customers or standing fat and watchful behind their displays.

In his extremity, the fruit beckoned with the promise of sanctuary for a few parts of him, but the integrating totality of him knew the emptiness of that thought. He fought off the lure, shuffled fast as he dared, dodging past customers, through the knots of idlers.

"You like to buy fresh oranges?"

An oily dark hand thrust two oranges into his face.

"Fresh oranges from the green country. Never been a bug near these."

He avoided the hand, but the odor of the oranges came near to overpowering him.

Now he was clear of the stalls, around a corner down a narrow side street. Another corner and he saw far away to his left the lure of greenery in open country, the free area beyond the town.

He turned toward the green, increased his speed, measuring out the time still available to him. He knew it would be a near thing. Poison clung to his clothing, but clean air filtered through the fabric—and the thought of possible victory was like an antidote.

We can make it yet!

The green drew closer and closer—trees and ferns beside a river bank. He heard running water, smelled wet soil. There was a bridge thronging with foot traffic from converging streets.

No help for it—he joined the throng, avoided contact where possible. His leg and back linkages were beginning to slip, and he knew the wrong kind of blow, a chance collision, could dislodge whole segments.

The bridge ordeal ended and he saw a dirt track leading off the path to the right and down toward the river. He turned toward it, stumbled against one of two men carrying a pig in a net slung between them. Part of the skin simulation on his right upper leg gave way. He could feel it begin to slip down inside his trousers.

The man he'd hit took two backward steps, almost dropped the pig.

"Careful!" the man shouted.

The man's companion said, "Damn drunks."

The pig set up a squirming, squealing distraction.

In this moment, he slipped past the men onto the dirt track, shuffled toward the river. He could see water down there now boiling with aeration from the barrier filters, the foam of sonic disruption on its surface.

Behind him, one of the pig carriers said, "I don't think he was drunk, Carlos. His skin felt dry and hot. Maybe he was sick."

He heard and understood, tried to increase his speed. The lost segment of skin simulation had slipped halfway down his leg. A disruptive loosening of shoulder and back muscles threatened his balance.

The track turned around an embankment of raw dirt dark brown with dampness and dipped into a tunnel through ferns and bushes. The men with the pig no longer could see him, he knew. He grabbed at his trousers where the leg surface was slipping, scurried through the green tunnel.

Where the tunnel ended he caught sight of his first mutated bee. It was dead, having entered this barrier vibration area without any protection against that deadliness. The bee was one of the butterfly type with irridescent yellow and orange wings. It lay in the cup of a green leaf at the center of a shaft of sunlight.

He shuffled past, having recorded the bee's shape and color. His kind had considered the bees as a possible way, but there were serious drawbacks. A bee could not reason with humans. And humans had to listen to reason soon, else all life would end.

There came the sound of someone hurrying down the path behind him. Heavy footsteps pounded the earth.

Pursuit?

Why would they pursue? Have I been discovered?

A sensation akin to panic fluttered through him, lent

his parts a burst of energy. But he was reduced to slow shuffling and soon it would be only a crawling progress. Every eye he could use searched the greenery for a place of concealment.

A thin break darkened the fern wall on his left. Tiny human footprints led into it—children. He forced his way through the ferns there, found himself on a low narrow path along the embankment. Two toy aircars, red and blue, lay abandoned on the path. His staggering foot pressed into the dirt.

The low path led close to a wall of black dirt festooned with creepers. It turned sharply as the dirt wall turned and emerged onto the lip of a shallow cave. More toys lay in the green gloom at the cave's mouth.

He knelt, crawled over the toys into the blessed dankness, lay there waiting.

Presently, the pounding footsteps hurried past a few meters below. Voices reached up to him.

"He was headed for the river. Think he was going to jump in?"

"Who knows? But I think me for sure he was sick."

"Here! Down this way; somebody's been down this way."

The voices grew indistinct, blended with the bubbling sound of water.

The men were going on down the path. They had missed his hiding place. But why had they pursued? He hadn't seriously injured that man. Surely they didn't suspect.

But speculation had to wait.

Slowly, he steeled himself for what had to be done, brought his specialized parts into play and began burrowing into the earth of the cave. Deeper and deeper he burrowed, thrusting the excess dirt behind and out to make it appear the cave had collapsed.

Ten meters in he went before stopping. His store of energy contained just enough reserve for the next stage. He turned onto his back, scattering the dead parts of legs and back, exposing the queen and her guard cluster to the dirt beneath his chitinous spine. Orifices opened at his thigh, exuded the cocoon foam, the soothing green cover that would harden into a protective shell.

This was victory; the essential parts had survived.

Time was the thing now—some twenty days to gather new energy, go through the metamorphosis and disperse. Soon there'd be thousands of him—each with its carefully mimicked clothing and identification papers, each with this appearance of humanity.

Identical—each of them.

There'd be other checkpoints, but not as severe; other barriers—lesser ones.

This human copy had proved to be a good one. The supreme integration of his kind had chosen well. They'd learned much from study of scattered captives in the *sertao*. But it was so difficult to understand the human creature. Even when they were permitted a limited freedom, it was almost impossible to reason with them. Their supreme integration eluded all attempts at contact.

And always the primary question remained: How could any supreme integration permit the disaster that was overtaking this entire planet?

Difficult humans—their slavery to the planet would have to be proved to them . . . dramatically, perhaps.

The queen stirred near the cool dirt, prodded into action by her guards. Unifying communication went out to all the body parts, seeking the survivors, assessing strengths. They'd learned new things this time about escaping notice from humans. All the subsequent colony clusters would share that knowledge. One of them at least would get through to the city by the Amazon "River Sea" where the death-for-all appeared to originate.

One of them had to get through.

2

Pastel smokes drifted on the cabaret's air. Each smoke, the signature of a table, wafted upward from a table's central vent—here a pale mauve, across the way a pink as delicate as baby skin, there a green that brought to mind Indian gauze woven of pampas grass. It had just turned 9:00 P.M. and the *Cabaret A'Chigua*, Bahia's finest, had begun its nightly entertainment. Tinkling bell music set a sensuous rhythm for a troupe of dancers posturing in stylized ant costumes. Their fake antennae and mandibles waved through the smokes.

A'Chigua's patrons occupied low divans. The women were a sprinkling of tropical color as rich as jungle flowers arranged against men in white linen and, here and there like punctuation marks, the glistening white smocks of bandeirantes. This was the Green area, where bandeirantes could relax and play after duty in the Red jungle or at the barriers.

Shoptalk and smalltalk in a dozen languages flowed through the room—

"Tonight I take a pink table for luck. It is the color of a woman's breast, no?" "So I laid down a blanket of foamal and we went in and cleaned out the whole nest—mutated ants like they had in the Piratininga. Must've been ten, twenty billion of them right there."

Dr. Rhin Kelly had listened to the room for twenty minutes, her attention drawn more and more to the tension undercurrents here.

"The new poisons work—yes." That was a bandeirante at the table behind her answering the problem of survivors—resistant strains. The mop-up is going to be brutal handwork, just like China. They had to get down there and kill the last bugs by hand."

Rhin sensed her companion stirring, and thought: *He heard.* She glanced up from their table's amber smoke, met her escort's almond eyes. He smiled and she thought as she had many times before what a distinguished *personage* was this Dr. Travis Huntington Chen-Lhu. He was tall with the deep, square face of North China topped by close-cropped hair that was still jet black at sixty. He leaned toward her and whispered, "Nowhere do we escape rumors, eh?"

She shook her head, wondering for perhaps the tenth time why the distinguished Dr. Chen-Lhu, district director for the International Ecological Organization, had insisted she come here tonight, her first night in Bahia. She had no illusions at all about why he'd ordered her to come down from Dublin: he obviously had a problem which required action by the IEO's espionage arm. As usual, the problem would turn out to involve a man who must be manipulated. Chen-Lhu had hinted as much during the day's "general briefing." But he had yet to name the man upon whom she must ply her wiles.

"They say certain plants are dying out from lack of pollenization." That was a woman at the table behind her, and Rhin stiffened. Dangerous conversation, that.

But the bandeirante directly behind her said, "Back off, doll. You sound like that dame they picked up in Itabuna."

"What *dame*?"

"She was distributing Carsonite literature right there in the village behind the barrier. Police grabbed her before she'd gotten rid of twenty pieces. They got most of it back, but you know how that stuff is, especially up there near the Red."

A disturbance erupted at *A'Chigua's* entrance, cries of "Johnny! You, Johnny! You lucky dog, Joao!"

Rhin joined the rest of *A'Chigua's* patrons in turning to stare toward the sound, noting that Chen-Lhu pretended indifference. She saw that seven bandeirantes had stopped just inside the room as though blocked by the barrage of words.

At their head stood a bandeirante with a group leader's golden butterfly insignia at his lapel. Rhin studied him with sudden suspicion, seeing a man of medium height, swarthy skin, wavy black hair; stocky, but when he moved there was grace. His body radiated strength. The face was a contrast, narrow and patrician, dominated by a slim nose with pronounced hook. There were *senhores de engenho* in his ancestry—obviously.

Rhin described him to herself as "brutally handsome." Again, she noted Chen-Lhu's pose of disinterest, and thought: *So this is why we're here.*

The thought made her oddly aware of her own body. She underwent a momentary revulsion at her role, thinking: *I've done many things and sold many bits of myself to be here in this moment. And what is there left for myself?* No one wanted the services of Dr. Rhin Kelly, entomologist. But Rhin Kelly, Irish beauty, a woman who took pleasure in her *other* duties—this Rhin Kelly was much in demand.

If I didn't enjoy the work, perhaps then I wouldn't hate it, she thought.

She knew how she must appear in this room of lush, dark-skinned women. She was red-haired, green-eyed, delicate complexion—freckles at shoulders, forehead and bridge of nose. In this room—wearing a low gown to match her eyes, a small golden IEO badge at her breast—in this room, she was the exotic one.

"Who is that man at the door?" she asked.

A smile like the ripple from a faint breeze washed over Chen-Lhu's chisled features. He glanced toward the entrance.

"Which man, my dear? There appear to be . . . seven there."

"Drop the pose, Travis."

Almond eyes probed at her, swung back to the group at the entrance. "That is Joao Martinho, *jefe* of the Irmandades and son of Gabriel Martinho."

"Joao Martinho," she said. "He's the one you said should've had full credit for clearing the Piratininga."

"He got the cash, my dear. For Johnny Martinho, that's quite enough."

"How much?"

"Ah, the practical woman," he said. "They shared five hundred thousand cruzados." Chen-Lhu settled back on the divan, sniffed the pungent incense arising with the smoke from their table's vent. And he thought: *Five hundred thousand! That'll be enough to destroy Johnny Martinho—if I can make my case against him. And with Rhin, how can I fail? This branco de Bahia will be only too happy to accept a woman as fair as Rhin. Yes. We'll have our scapegoat soon: Johnny Mar-*

tinho, the capitalisto, the gran senhor who was trained by the Yankees.

"The grapevine in Dublin mentions Joao Martinho," Rhin said.

"Ahh, the grapevine," he said. "What has it said?"

"The trouble in the Piratininga—his name and that of his father are mentioned."

"Ahhh, I see."

"There are strange rumors," she said.

"And you find them sinister."

"No—just odd."

Odd, he thought. The word struck him with a momentary sinking sensation because it echoed the courier message from his homeland that had moved him to send for Rhin. *"Your odd slowness in solving our problem is causing very disturbing questions to be raised."* The sentence and the word had leaped out of the message. Chen-Lhu understood the impatience that framed those words: discovery of the looming catastrophe in China could come at any moment. And he knew there were those who didn't trust him because of the cursed white men in his ancestry.

He lowered his voice, said, "Odd is not quite the word to describe bandeirantes reinfesting the Green areas."

"I heard some rather wild stories," she murmured. "Secret bandeirante laboratories—illegal mutation experiments . . ."

"You'll note, Rhin, that most reports of strange, giant insects come from bandeirantes. There's your only oddity."

"Logical," she said. "Bandeirantes're out in the front line where such things might occur."

"Surely you, an entomologist, don't believe such wild stories," he said.

She shrugged, feeling oddly perverse. He was right, of course; had to be.

"Logic," Chen-Lhu said. "The use of wild rumors to foment superstitious fear among the yokel *tabareus*, this is the only logic I see."

"So you wish me to work on this bandeirante chief," she said. "What am I supposed to find?"

You're supposed to find what I tell you to find, Chen-Lhu thought. But he said, "Why're you so certain this Martinho is your target? Is that what the grapevine said?"

"Ohhh," she said, wondering at the anger that lurked within her. "You had no special purpose in sending for me. My own charming self was reason enough!"

"I couldn't have said it better," he said. He turned, beckoned a waiter who approached, bent to listen. Presently, the waiter wove a path to the group at the entrance, spoke to Joao Martinho.

The bandeirante studied Rhin with a brief flicker, shifted to meet Chen-Lhu's eyes. Chen-Lhu nodded.

Several women like gauze butterflies had joined Martinho's group. Eye makeup made them appear to be staring from faceted pits. Martinho disengaged himself, headed for the table of amber smoke. He stopped across from Rhin, bowed to Chen-Lhu. "Dr. Chen-Lhu, I presume," he said. "What a delight. How can the IEO spare its district director for such dalliance?" The wave of an arm encompassed *A'Chigua's* frenetic tensions.

And Martinho thought: *There—I've spoken my thoughts in a way this devious man will understand.*

"I indulge myself," Chen-Lhu said. "A small bit of relaxation to welcome a newcomer to our staff." He arose from the divan, looked down at Rhin. "Rhin, I'd like you to meet Senhor Joao Martinho. Johnny, this is

Dr. Rhin Kelly, late of Dublin, a new entomologist in our office."

And Chen-Lhu thought: *This is the enemy. Make no mistake. This is the enemy. This is the enemy. This is the enemy.*

Martinho bowed from the hips. "Charmed."

"It's an honor to meet you, Senhor Martinho," she said. "I've heard of your exploits ... even in Dublin."

"Even in Dublin," he murmured. "I was favored, but never so much favored as in this instant." He stared at her with disconcerting intensity, wondering what special duties this woman might have. Was she Chen-Lhu's mistress?

Into the sudden silence came the voice of a woman at the table behind Rhin: "Snakes and rodents *are* increasing their pressures on civilization. It says so in the ..."

Someone shushed her.

Martinho said, "Travis, I do not understand it. How can one call such a beautiful woman Doctor?"

Chen-Lhu forced a chuckle. "Careful, Johnny. Dr. Kelly is my new field director."

"A roving director, I hope," Martinho said.

Rhin stared at him coolly, but it was an assumed coolness. She found his directness exciting and frightening. "I've been warned about Latin blandishments," she said. "You've all hidden a piece of the blarney stone in your family trees, so I've been told."

Her voice had taken on a rich throatiness which made Chen-Lhu smile to himself. *Remember—this is the enemy,* he thought. "Will you join us, Johnny?" he asked.

"You save me from forcing myself upon you," Martinho said. "But you know I've some of my Irmandades with me?"

"They appear to be occupied," Chen-Lhu said. He nodded toward the entrance, where a cluster of the gauzy women had enfolded all but one of Martinho's companions. Women and bandeirantes were finding seats at a large blue-vent table in a corner.

The lone holdout shifted his attention from Martinho to his companions at the table, back to Martinho.

Rhin studied the man: ash-gray hair, a long young-old face marred by an acid scar on the left cheek. He reminded her of the sexton in her Wexford church.

"Ah, that is Vierho," Martinho said. "We call him the Padre. At the moment, he is undecided who to protect—our brothers of the Irmandades over there or myself. Me, I think I need him most." He beckoned to Vierho, turned, sat down beside Rhin.

A waiter appeared, slipped a translucent bulb containing a golden drink onto the table in front of him. A glass tube protruded from the bulb. He ignored it, stared at Rhin.

"Are the Irish ready to join us?" he asked.

"Join you?"

"In realignment of the world's insects."

She glanced at Chen-Lhu, whose face betrayed no reaction to the question, returned her attention to Martinho. "The Irish share the reluctance of the Canadians and the North Americans of the United States. The Irish will wait a bit yet."

The answer appeared to annoy him. "But . . . I mean Ireland surely understands the advantages," he said. "You've no snakes. That must . . ."

"That's something God did by the hand of St. Patrick," she said. "I don't fancy the bandeirantes as cast in the same mold." She'd spoken in quick anger and regretted it immediately.

"I should've warned you, Johnny," Chen-Lhu said.

"She has an Irish temper." And he thought: *He's putting on an act for my benefit—devious little man.*

"I see," Martinho said. "If God didn't see fit to rid us of insects, perhaps we're wrong in trying to do this for ourselves."

Rhin glared at him in dismay.

Chen-Lhu suppressed a surge of pure rage. *That devious Latin maneuvered Rhin into this position! Deliberately!*

"My government doesn't recognize the existence of God," Chen-Lhu said. "Perhaps if God were to initiate an exchange of embassies . . ." He patted Rhin's arm, noted that she was trembling. "However, the IEO believes we'll be extending the fight north of the Rio Grande Line within ten years."

"The IEO believes this? Or is it China's belief?"

"Both," Chen-Lhu said.

"Even if the North Americans object?"

"They are expected to see the light of reason."

"And the Irish?"

Rhin managed a smile. "The Irish," she said, "have always been notoriously unreasonable." She reached for her drink, hesitated as her attention was caught by a white-clad bandeirante standing across the table—Vierho.

Martinho bounced to his feet, bowed once more to Rhin. "*Doctor* Kelly, allow me to introduce one of my brothers of the Irmandades, Padre Vierho." He turned back to Rhin. "This lovely one, my esteemed Padre, is a *field* director of the IEO."

Vierho gave her a tight little nod, sat down stiffly at the limit of the divan beyond Chen-Lhu. "Charmed," he murmured.

"My Irmandades, they are shy," Martinho said. He

resumed his seat beside Rhin. "They'd rather be out killing ants."

"Johnny, how is your father?" Chen-Lhu asked.

Martinho spoke without looking away from Rhin. "The affairs of the Mato Grosso keep him much occupied." He paused. "You have lovely eyes."

Again, Rhin found herself disconcerted by his directness. She picked up the golden bulb of his drink, said, "What is this?"

"Ah, that is flierce, the Brazilian mead. Take it for yourself. There are little points of light in your eyes to match the gold of the drink."

She suppressed a quick retort, lifted the drink to sip it, genuinely curious. She stopped with the glass tube almost at her lips as she caught Vierho staring at her hair.

"Is it really that color?" he asked.

Martinho laughed, a surprised and oddly affectionate sound. "Ahh, Padre," he said.

Rhin sipped the drink to cover a feeling of confusion, found the liquid softly sweet, filled with the memory of many flowers, and with a sharp bite beneath the sugar.

"But is it that color?" Vierho insisted.

Chen-Lhu leaned forward. "Many Irish colleens have such red hair, Vierho. It's supposed to signify a wild temper."

Rhin returned the drink to the table, wondering at her own emotions. She sensed a camaraderie between Vierho and his chief and resented the fact that she couldn't share it.

"Where next, Johnny?" Chen-Lhu asked.

Martinho darted a glance at his brother Irmandade, returned a hard stare to Chen-Lhu. *Why does this official of the IEO ask such a question here and now?* he wondered. *Chen-Lhu must know where next. It could not be otherwise.*

"I'm surprised you hadn't heard," Martinho said. "This afternoon I bid-in the Serra Dos Parecis."

"By the great bug of the Mambuca," Vierho muttered.

Anger showed in the sudden darkening of Martinho's face. "Vierho!" he snapped.

Rhin stared from one to the other. A strange silence had settled over the table. She felt it as a tingling along her arms and shoulders. There was something about it that was fearful, even sexual . . . and profoundly disturbing. She recognized the reaction of her body, hated it, knew she could not place its source with any precision this time. All she could say to herself was: *This is why Chen-Lhu sent for me—to attract this Joao Martinho and manipulate him. I'll do it, but what I'll hate most is the fact that I'll enjoy it.*

"But, Jefe," Vierho said. "You know yourself what was said about . . ."

"I know!" Martinho barked. "Yes!"

Vierho nodded, a look of pain on his face. "They said it was . . ."

"There are mutants, we know that," Martinho said. And he thought: *Why did Chen-Lhu force this disclosure now? To see me argue with one of my men?*

"Mutants?" Chen-Lhu asked.

"We have seen what we have seen," Vierho said.

"But the description of this *thing* is a physical impossibility," Martinho said. "It has to be a product of someone's superstition. *That* I know."

"Do you, Jefe?"

"Anything that's there we can face," Martinho said.

"What *are* you talking about?" Rhin asked.

Chen-Lhu cleared his throat. *Let her see now the ex-*

tremes to which our enemy will go, he thought. *Let her see the perfidy of these bandeirantes. Then, when I tell her what she must do, she'll do it willingly.*

"There is a story, Rhin," Chen-Lhu said.

"Story!" Martinho sneered.

"Rumor, then," Chen-Lhu said. "Some of the bandeirantes of Diogo Alvarez say they saw a mantidae three meters tall in the Serra Dos Parecis."

Vierho leaned toward Chen-Lhu, face tense. The acid scar was pale on the bandeirante's cheek. "Alvarez lost six men before he gave up the Serra. You know that, Senhor? Six men! And he . . ."

Vierho broke off at the arrival of a squat, dark-skinned man in a stained bandeirante working smock. The man was round faced, with Indian eyes. He stopped almost behind Martinho, stood there waiting.

The newcomer bent close to Martinho, whispered.

Rhin could catch only a few of his words—they were very low and in some barbarous interlands dialect—something about the Plaza, the central square . . . crowds.

Martinho pursed his lips, said, "When?"

Ramon straightened, spoke somewhat louder. "Just now, Jefe."

"In the Plaza?"

"Yes—less than a block from here."

"What is it?" Chen-Lhu asked.

"A namesake of this cabaret," Martinho said.

"A chigger?"

"So they say."

"But this area's Green," Rhin said. And she wondered at her sudden feelings of dismay.

Martinho pushed himself up and away from the divan.

Chen-Lhu's face betrayed a strange watchfulness as he looked up at the bandeirante jefe.

"You will excuse me, please, Rhin Kelly?" Martinho asked.

"Where are you going?" she asked.

"There is work."

"One chigger?" Chen-Lhu asked. "Are you sure it isn't a mistake?"

"No mistake, senhor," Ramon said.

"Is there no facility for taking care of such accidents, then?" Rhin asked. "Obviously we've a stowaway that's come into the Green on some sort of cargo or . . ."

"Perhaps not," Martinho said. He nodded to Vierho. "Get the men. I will need especially Thome for the truck and Lon to manage the lights."

"At once, Jefe." Vierho bounced up and headed across the room toward the other Irmandades.

"What do you mean—*perhaps not?*" Chen-Lhu asked.

"This is one of the new ones about which you refuse, to believe," Martinho said. He turned to Ramon. "Go with Vierho, please."

"Yes, Jefe."

Ramon turned with an almost military precision, strode in Vierho's wake.

"You will explain, please?" Chen-Lhu said.

"This is described as an acid-shooter and almost a half meter long," Martinho said.

"Impossible!" Chen-Lhu snorted.

Rhin shook her head. "No chigger could possibly . . ."

"This is a bandeirante joke," Chen-Lhu said.

"As you wish, senhor," Martinho said. "You have seen the acid scar on Vierho's cheek? This too was produced by such a joke." He turned, bowed to Rhin. "Your forgiveness, Senhorita?"

Rhin stood up. *A chigger almost half a meter long!*

The odd rumors she'd heard half a world away reached out and touched her now, filling her with a sense of unreality. There were physical limits. Such a thing could not be. Or could it? She was all entomologist now. Logic and training took over. This was a matter which might be proved or disproved in just a few minutes. Less than a block away, the man had said. In the Plaza. And certainly Chen-Lhu wouldn't want her to disengage herself from Joao Martinho quite this early.

"We are going with you, of course," she said.

"Of course," Chen-Lhu said, rising.

Rhin slipped an arm beneath Martinho's. "Show me this fantastic chigger, if you please, Senhor Martinho."

Martinho placed a hand over hers, felt an electric sensation of warmth. *What a disturbing woman!* "Please," he said. "You are so lovely, and the thought of what the acid of this . . ."

"I'm certain we'll be quite safe from a rumor," Chen-Lhu said. "Will you lead the way, please, Johnny?"

Martinho sighed. The unbelievers were so stubborn—but this was a chance to reach into a high place with inescapable evidence of what most bandeirantes already knew. Yes; District Director Chen-Lhu should come. Indeed, he must come. Reluctantly, Martinho transferred Rhin's arm to Chen-Lhu. "Of course you will come," he said. "But please keep the lovely Rhin Kelly well to the rear, Senhor. Rumors sometimes develop a terrible sting."

"We will take every necessary precaution," Chen-Lhu said. The jibe in his voice was quite apparent.

Martinho's men already were headed for the door.

He turned, strode after them, ignoring the abrupt hush of the room as attention followed him.

Rhin, accompanying Chen-Lhu toward the street, was struck by the purposeful set to the bandeirantes' shoulders. They did not appear like men bent on deception— but that was what it must be. It couldn't be anything else.

3

The night was a blue-white glare from slave lights hanging in their carrier beams above the street. People in the costumes of many nations and many regions, a multi-colored river of people, flowed past the *A'Chigua* toward the Plaza.

Martinho sped up, led his men into the stream. People made way; words of recognition followed.

"It's Joao Martinho and some of his Irmandades."

". . . the Piratininga with Benito Alvarez."

"Joao Martinho . . ."

At the Plaza, a white truck of the Hermosillo Bandeirantes played its searchlights on the fountain. There were other trucks and official vehicles across the way. The Hermosillo truck was a working rig recently returned from the interlands, by the look of it. The interleavings of its extensile wings were still streaked with dirt. The break-line of its forward pod could be distinguished clearly—a distinct crack that ran completely around the vehicle. Two of its ground-lift pods didn't quite match the white of the others, evidence of a field repair job.

Martinho followed the pointing fingers of the search-lights. He moved forward to a line of police and ban-deirantes holding back the crowd, was passed through on recognition, his men following.

"Where's Ramon?" Martinho asked.

Vierho pressed up close beside him, said, "Ramon went for the truck with Thome and Lon. I don't see a'chigua."

"But look you," Martinho said, pointing.

The crowd was being held back all around the Plaza at a distance of about fifty meters from the central foun-tain which rose in spooling, glistening arcs. In front of the crowd lay a tiled circle, its mosaic surface decorated with figures of the birds of Brazil. Inside this tiled ring, a ten-centimeter lip lifted to a circle of green lawn about twenty meters in diameter with the fluted cup of the fountain in the center. Between tile and fountain the lawn showed yellow splotches of dead grass. Martinho's pointing finger picked out these patches one by one.

"Acid," Vierho whispered.

The searchlights centered abruptly on a shifting movement within the spray at the fountain's rim. A hiss-ing passed through the crowd like a sudden wind.

"And there it is," Martinho said. "Now, will the so-suspicious official of the IEO believe?"

As he spoke, a scintillant spray arched from the crea-ture at the fountain and out onto the lawn.

"*Eeee-ahhhh*," the crowd said.

Martinho grew conscious of a low moaning off to his left, turned to see a doctor being directed there along the inner rim of the crowd. The doctor turned into the crowd on the other side of the Hermosillo truck, lifting his bag over his head as he entered the press of people.

"Who was hurt?" Martinho asked.

One of the police behind him said, "It is Alvarez. He tried to get that . . . thing, but he took only a handshield and a sprayrifle. The shield was not proof against a'chigua's quickness. It got Alvarez in the arm."

Vierho tugged at Martinho's sleeve, pointed into the crowd behind the policeman. Rhin Kelly and Chen-Lhu were being passed through the onlookers there, space being made for them as people recognized the IEO insignia.

Rhin waved, called, "Senhor Martinho—that thing is impossible! It's at least seventy-five centimeters long. It must weigh three or four kilos."

"Do they not believe their own eyes?" Vierho asked.

Chen-Lhu came up to the policeman who'd described the injury to Alvarez, said, "Let us through, please."

"Eh? Oh . . . yes, sir." The line of guards parted.

Chen-Lhu stopped beside the bandeirante leader, glanced down at Rhin, back to Martinho. "I don't believe it, either. I'd give a pretty to get my hands on that . . . thing."

"What is it you don't believe?" Martinho asked.

"I think it's some kind of automaton. Not so, Rhin?"

"It has to be," she said.

"How much of a pretty would you give?" Martinho asked.

"Ten thousand cruzados."

"Please keep the lovely *Doctor* Kelly back here out of range," Martinho said. He turned to Vierho. "What's keeping Ramon and that truck? Find them. I want our magna-glass shield and a modified sprayrifle."

"Jefe!"

"At once. Oh, yes—and get a large specimen bottle."

Vierho sighed, turned away to obey.

"What do you say that thing is?" Chen-Lhu asked.

"I don't have to say."

"Do you imply it's one of the *things* which none but bandeirantes appear to see in the interlands?"

"I don't deny what my own eyes see."

"Why have *we* never seen specimens, I wonder?" Chen-Lhu mused.

Martinho swallowed to suppress an angry outburst. This fool safe back here in the Green! He dared to question what the bandeirantes knew for fact!

"Isn't that an interesting question?" Chen-Lhu asked.

"We've been lucky to get out with just our lives," Martinho growled.

"Any entomologist will tell you that thing's a physical impossibility," Rhin said.

"The material won't support such structure through that sort of activity," Chen-Lhu said.

"I can see the entomologists must be correct," Martinho said.

Rhin stared up at him. The angry cynicism surprised her. He attacked and did not remain on the defensive. He acted like a man who believed that *impossibility* out there at the fountain actually was a giant insect. But in the night club he'd argued the other side.

"You've seen such things in the jungle?" Chen-Lhu asked.

"Did you not see the scar on Vierho's face?"

"What does a scar prove?"

"We have seen . . . what we have seen."

"But an insect cannot grow that large!" Rhin protested. She turned her attention to the dark creature dancing along the fountain's rim behind the curtain of water.

"So I've been told," Martinho said. He wondered then about the reports from the Serra Dos Parecis.

Mantidae three meters tall—ten feet. He knew the argument against such a thing. Rhin—all the entomologists were correct. Insects couldn't produce living structure that large. Was it possible the things were automata? Who'd build such things? Why?

"It has to be a mechanical simulation of some kind," Rhin said.

"The acid's real, though," Chen-Lhu said. "Look at the yellow spots on the lawn."

Martinho reminded himself then that his own basic training forced him to agree with Rhin and Chen-Lhu. He'd even denied to Vierho that giant mantidae could exist. He knew how rumors pyramided. There were so few people other than bandeirantes in the Red areas these days. The Resettlement Plan had been most efficient. And there was no denying that many bandeirantes were semi-ignorant, superstitious men attracted only by the romance and money.

Martinho shook his head. He'd been there on the Goyaz track the day Vierho had suffered the acid burn. He'd seen . . . what he had seen. And now, this creature at the fountain.

The high-pitched roaring hiss of truck motors intruded on his awareness. The sound grew louder. The crowd parted giving a wide berth to the ground blast as Ramon backed the Irmandades truck into position beside the Hermosillo vehicle. The rear doors opened and Vierho jumped down as the motors were silenced.

"Jefe," he called. "Why do we not use the truck? Ramon could put it almost up to the . . ."

Martinho waved him to silence, spoke to Chen-Lhu: "The truck does not have enough maneuverability. You saw how fast that thing is."

"You haven't said what you think it is," Chen-Lhu said.

"I'll say when I see it in a specimen bottle," Martinho said.

Vierho came up beside him, said, "But the truck would give us . . ."

"No! Dr. Chen-Lhu desires an undamaged specimen. Get us some foam bombs. We go in with our hands."

Vierho sighed, shrugged, returned to the rear of the truck, spoke briefly to someone inside. A bandeirante in the truck began passing out equipment.

Martinho turned to the policeman helping hold back the crowd, said, "Can you get a message to the vehicles across the way?"

"Of course, honorable sir."

"I want their lights turned off. I don't want to risk being blinded by lights in front of me. You understand?"

"They will be told at once." He turned, relayed the message to an officer down the line.

Martinho strode to the rear of his truck, took a spray-rifle, examined the charge cylinder, extracted it, took another from a door rack. He locked in the charge, and again checked the rifle.

"Keep the specimen bottle here until we've immobilized that . . . thing," he said. "I'll call for it."

Vierho rolled out the shield, a two-centimeter thickness of acid-resistant, tempered magna-glass, mounted on a two-wheeled handtruck. A narrow slot at the right accepted the rifle.

A bandeirante in the truck handed out two protective suits—silver-gray fiberglass sandwiches encased in slick acid-resistant synthetic fabric.

Martinho slipped into one, examined the seals.

Vierho donned the other.

"I could use Thome on the shield," Martinho said.

"Thome has not as much experience, Jefe."

Martinho nodded, began examining the foamal bombs and auxiliary equipment. He hung extra charge cylinders in a rack on the shield.

It was all done quickly and silently, with the ease of long experience. The crowd behind the truck took on some of their silence—a charged waiting. Only the faintest murmuring of conversation surrounded the truck.

"It is still there on the fountain, Jefe," Vierho said.

He took the control handle of the shield, moved it out onto the mosaic tiles. The right wheel stopped on the patterned blue-scale neck of a condor worked into the tiles. Martinho rested his sprayrifle in its slot, said, "This'd be easier if we only had to kill it."

"Those things are quick as O Diablo," Vierho said. "I do not like this, Jefe. If that thing should get around our shield . . ." He fingered the sleeve of his protective suit. "This would be like a piece of gauze trying to stop the river."

"So don't let it get around the shield."

"I will do my best, Jefe."

Martinho studied the creature waiting behind the water curtain at the rim of the fountain, said, "Bring a handlight. Perhaps we can dazzle it."

Vierho set the shield stand, returned to the truck. He was back in a moment with the light hanging from his belt.

"Let's go," Martinho said.

Vierho released the handtruck stand, activated its motors. A faint humming issued from it. He turned the driver handle two notches. The shield crept forward, levered its way over the raised ring of the Plaza onto the lawn.

A stream of acid arched outward from the creature at the fountain, splashed onto the grass ten meters in front of them. Oily white smoke boiled from the lawn, was dispersed to their left by a light breeze. Martinho noted the direction of the breeze, signaled for the shield to be turned upwind. They circled right.

Another stream of acid arched toward them, fell short about the same distance.

"It is trying to tell us something, Jefe," Vierho joked.

Slowly they approached it, crossed one of the yellowed patches of grass.

Again the stream lifted from the fountain rim. Vierho leaned the shield backward. Acid splashed onto the glass, ran down the front. A biting smell filled their nostrils.

A murmurous *"Ahhhhhhhh"* lifted from the crowd around the Plaza.

"They are fools to stand that close, you know," Vierho said. "If that thing should charge . . ."

"Someone would shoot it with a hard-pellet," Martinho said. "Fini a'chigua."

"Fini Dr. Chen-Lhu's specimen," Vierho said. "Fini ten thousand cruzados."

"Yes," Martinho said. "We must not forget why we run this risk."

"I hope you don't believe I'd do this for love," Vierho said. He inched the shield forward another meter.

A foggy area began to form where the acid had hit.

"Etched the magna-glass!" Vierho said, astonishment filling his voice.

"Smelled something like Oxalic," Martinho said. "Must be stronger, though. Take it slow now. I want a sure shot."

"Why don't you try a foam bomb?"

"Vierho!"

"Ahhh, yes: the water."

The creature began sliding to their right along the fountain. Vierho turned the shield to cover this new approach. The creature stopped, retraced its steps.

"Wait a bit," Martinho said. He found a clear place in the glass, studied the thing.

The creature shifted back and forth, plainly visible on the fountain rim. It resembled its tiny namesake the way a caricature might. Its sectioned body appeared to be supported on ribbed legs that bowed outward to terminate in strong, gripping hairs. The antennae were stubby and glistened wetly at the ends.

Abruptly, it lifted a tubular nose, squirted a hard stream directly at the shield.

Martinho ducked involuntarily. "We must get closer," he said. "It must not have time to recover after I stun it."

"With what have you charged the rifle, Jefe?"

"Our special mix—dilute sulphur and corrosive sublimate in air-coagulating butyl carrier. I want to tangle its legs."

"I wish you had also brought something to plug its nose."

"Come along, old gray head," Joao said.

Vierho urged the shield closer, bent to peer past the acid fogging.

The giant chigger danced sideways, turned, darted off to the right along the fountain rim. Abruptly, it whirled, arched a stream of acid at them. The liquid glistened under the searchlights like a high curve of jewels. Vierho barely had time to swerve the shield into the new attack.

"By the blood of ten thousand saints," Vierho muttered. "I do not like working in this close to such a thing, Jefe. We are not fighters of bulls."

"This is no bull, my brother. It hasn't the horns."

"I think I would prefer the horns."

"We talk too much," Martinho said. "Closer, eh?"

Vierho urged the shield ahead until a bare two meters separated them from the creature on the fountain. "Shoot it," he hissed.

"We will get only one shot," Martinho said. "I must not damage the specimen. The Doctor wishes a whole specimen."

And he thought: *So do I.*

He swung the rifle toward the creature, but the chigger leaped to the lawn, back to the fountain rim. A scream lifted from the crowd.

Martinho and Vierho crouched, watching as their prey danced back and forth.

"Why doesn't it stand still for just a second?" Martinho asked.

"Jefe, if it comes under the shield, we are cooked. Why do you wait? Pick it off."

"I must be certain of it," Martinho said.

He swung the sprayrifle back and forth with the motions of the darting, dancing insect. It dodged away from the line of sight each time, moving farther and farther to the right. Suddenly, it turned, scuttled on around the fountain's rim to the opposite side. Now the entire water curtain separated them from it, but the searchlights had followed the retreat and they could still see it there.

Martinho entertained the odd suspicion then that the thing was trying to maneuver them into some special position. He lifted his suit's face shield, wiped his forehead with his left hand. He was perspiring heavily. It was a hot night, but here by the fountain there was cool mist in the air—and the bitter smell of the acid.

"I think we are in trouble," Vierho said. "If it keeps the fountain between us, how will we capture it?"

"Come along," Martinho said. "If it stays across the fountain from us, I'll order out another team. It cannot dodge two teams."

Vierho began maneuvering the shield sideways around the fountain. "I still think we should've used the truck," he said.

"Too big and clumsy," Martinho said. "Besides, I think the truck might frighten it into attempting a break through the crowd. This way, it may feel it has a chance against us."

"Jefe, I feel that same thing."

The giant chigger took this moment to dart toward them, stop and crawl backwards. It kept its nose aimed at the shield and presented a steady target, but too much of the water curtain fell between it and Martinho for a safe shot.

"The wind is at our backs, Jefe," Vierho said.

"I know. Let's hope that thing hasn't the wit to shoot over our heads. The wind'd drop acid onto our backs."

The chigger backed into an area where the fountain's upper structure shadowed it from the searchlights. It shifted back and forth in the shadow area, a dark wet movement.

"Jefe, that thing is not going to stay there for long. I can feel it."

"Hold the shield here a moment," Martinho said. "I think you're right. We ought to clear the Plaza. If it took it into its mind to rush the crowd, people would be hurt."

"You say a true thing, Jefe."

"Vierho, use the handlight. Try to dazzle its eyes. I'll break away from the shield to our right and try a long shot."

"Jefe!"

"You have a better idea?"

"At least let us pull the shield farther out there into the lawn. You would not be so close if . . ."

Still in the shadows, the chigger hopped sideways off the fountain rim onto the lawn. Vierho jerked up the handlight, bathed the creature in a blue-white glare.

"O, Dios, Jefe! Shoot it!"

Martinho swung the sprayrifle around to bear on the new position, but the shield slot prevented a full swing. He cursed, grabbed for the control handle, but before he could swing the shield, a section of lawn the size of a street man-hole lifted like a trapdoor behind the chigger and in the full glare of the handlight. A black shape with what appeared to be a triple-horned head emerged partly from the hole, sounded a rasping call.

The chigger darted past the shape and into the hole.

The crowd was screaming now, a noise compounded of rage, fear and feral excitement that filled the air of the Plaza. Through it all, Martinho could hear Vierho praying in a low voice—almost a chant: "Holy Mary, Mother of God . . ."

Martinho tried to push the shield around toward the creature in the hole, was stalled by Vierho trying to pull the structure backward. The shield twisted around on its wheels, exposing them to the black shape there as the thing lifted another half meter onto the lawn. Martinho had a full, clear look at it there bathed in the beam of the handlight. The thing looked like a gigantic stag beetle—taller than a man and with triple horns.

Desperately, Martinho wrestled the sprayrifle from its shield slot, swung it toward the horned monster.

"Jefe, Jefe, Jefe!" Vierho pleaded.

Martinho brought his weapon to bear, squeezed off a two-second charge, counting to himself: "One butterfly, two butterfly."

The poison-butyl mixture slammed into the creature, enveloped it.

The creature, its shape distorted by the spray-mix, hesitated, then lifted farther out of the hole with a rasping, grunting sound heard clearly above the crowd screams.

The crowd fell abruptly silent as the thing towered there, a shell-backed monster—green, black, glistening— at least a meter taller than a man.

Martinho could hear a sucking, gasping sound from it, an odd wet noise like the sound of the fountain with which it competed.

Carefully, he again aimed the sprayrifle at the horned head—point blank range—and emptied the charge cylinder: ten seconds. The creature appeared to dissolve backward into its hole with eerie extensions and protrusions fighting the sticky butyl.

"Jefe, let us go away from here," Vierho pleaded. "Please, Jefe." He swung the shield around until it again stood between them and the giant insect. "Please," Vierho said. He began forcing Martinho back with the shield.

Martinho grabbed another charge cylinder, slammed it into his rifle, took a foamal bomb in his left hand. He felt emptied of every emotion except the need to attack that monster and kill it. But before he could draw his arm back to throw the bomb, he felt the shield buck. He looked up to a solid stream of liquid driving down on the shield from the black creature in the hole.

He needed no urging as Vierho screamed, "Run!"

They fled backward, dragging the shield.

The attack stopped as they drew out of range. Martinho stopped, looked back. He felt Vierho trembling beside him. The dark thing in the hole sank slowly backward. It was the most menacing retreat Martinho had ever seen. The movement radiated a willingness to return to the attack. It sank from sight. The section of lawn closed behind it.

As though that were the signal, the crowd sounds picked up all around the Plaza, but Martinho could hear the fear in the voices even when he couldn't make out the words.

He threw back his face shield, listening to the words like sharp cries, the snatches of sentences—"Like a monster beetle!" "Have you heard the report from the waterfront?" "The whole region could be infested!" "... at the Monte Ochoa Convent ... orphanage ..."

Through it all came the same question repeated from all sides of the Plaza: "What was it?" "What was it?" "What was it?"

Martinho felt someone at his right, jerked around to see Chen-Lhu standing there, eyes intent on the place where the beetle shape had disappeared. There was no sign of Rhin Kelly.

"Yes, Johnny," Chen-Lhu said. "What was it?"

"It looked like a giant stag beetle," Martinho said, and he was surprised at how calm his voice sounded.

"It was taller than a man by half," Vierho muttered. "Jefe ... those stories about the Serra dos Paresis ..."

"I heard the crowd talking about Monte Ochoa and the waterfront, something about an orphanage," Martinho said. "What was that?"

"Rhin has gone to investigate," Chen-Lhu said. "There are some disturbing reports. I'm having the crowd cleared out of the Plaza. People are being ordered to disperse and go to their homes."

"What are the disturbing reports?"

"That there has been some sort of tragedy at the waterfront and again at the Monte Ochoa Convent and orphanage."

"What sort of tragedy?"

"That is what Rhin's investigating."

"You saw that out there on the lawn," Martinho said. "Now will you believe what we've been reporting to you these many months?"

"I saw an acid-shooting automaton and a man in the costume of a stag beetle," Chen-Lhu said. "I'm curious to know if you were party to this deception."

Vierho cursed under his breath.

Martinho took a moment to put down his sudden anger, said only, "It didn't look to me like a man in costume." He shook his head. This was no time to let emotion cloud reason. *Insects could not possibly grow that large. The forces of gravity . . .* Again, he shook his head. *Then what was it?*

"We should at least get samples of the acid off the lawn there," Martinho said. "And that hole will have to be investigated."

"I've sent for our Security Section," Chen-Lhu said. He turned away, thinking of how he would have to compose the reports on this—the one for his superiors in the IEO and the special report for his own government.

"Did you see how it appeared to dissolve downward into the hole when I hit it with the spray?" Martinho asked. "That poison can be painful, Travis. A man would've screamed."

"A man in protective clothing," Chen-Lhu, speaking with out turning. But he began to wonder about Martinho. The man seemed genuinely puzzled. No matter. This whole incident was going to be useful. Chen-Lhu saw that now.

"But it came back out of the hole," Vierho said. "You saw that. It came back."

An abrupt growling sound came from the people being pushed out of the Plaza. It passed through them like a wind—voice to voice to voice.

Martinho turned, studied them. "Vierho," he said.

"Jefe?"

"Get blast-pellet carbines from the truck."

"At once, Jefe."

Vierho trotted across the lawn toward the truck which stood now in an open area with only a scattering of bandeirantes around it. Martinho recognized some of the men—those of Alvarez seemed most numerous, but there were bandeirantes also of the Hermosillo and Junitza.

"What do you want with blast-pellet weapons?" Chen-Lhu asked.

"I am going to look in that hole."

"My Security men will be here soon. We'll wait for them."

"I am going now."

"Martinho, I'm telling you that . . ."

"You are not the government of Brazil, Doctor. I am licensed by my government for a specific task. I am pledged to carry out that task wherever . . ."

"Martinho, if you destroy evidence of . . ."

"You were not out here facing those things, *Doctor*. You were safe back there at the Plaza's edge while I was earning the right to look in that hole."

Chen-Lhu's face grew rigid with anger, but he held himself silent until he knew he could control his voice, then said, "In that case, I will go with you now."

"As you wish."

Martinho turned away, stared across the Plaza to where the carbines were being handed out of the rear of his truck. Vierho collected them, headed back across the lawn. A tall, bald-headed Negro with right arm in a sling fell into step beside Vierho. The Negro wore a uniform of plain bandeirante white with the golden spray emblem of a band leader at his left shoulder. His craggy, Moorish features were drawn into a scowl of pain.

"There's Alvarez," Chen-Lhu said.

"I see him."

Chen-Lhu faced Martinho, assumed a rueful smile to match his tone. "Johnny—let us not fight. You know why the IEO assigned me to Brazil."

"I know. China's already completed the realignment of its insects. You're a big success."

"We've nothing but the mutated bees now, Johnny—not a single creature to spread disease or eat food intended for humans."

"I know, Travis. And you're here to make our job easier."

Chen-Lhu frowned at the tone of patient disbelief in Martinho's voice. He said, "Exactly."

"Then why won't you let our observers or those from the UN go in and see for themselves, Doctor?"

"Johnny! You certainly must know how long my country suffered under the white imperialists. Some of our people believe the danger's still there. They see spies everywhere."

"But you're more a man of the world, more understanding, eh, Travis?"

"Of course! My great grandmother was English, one of *the* Travis-Huntingtons. We have a tradition of broader understanding in my family."

"It's a wonder your country trusts you," Martinho said. "You're part white imperialist." He turned to greet Alvarez as the Negro stopped in front of them. "Hi, Benito. Sorry about your arm."

"Hullo, Johnny." Alvarez's voice was deep and rumbling. "God protected me. I will recover." He glanced down at the carbines in Vierho's hands, returned his attention to Martinho. "I heard the Padre here asking for blast-pellets. You could only want them for one reason."

"I have to look in that hole, Benito."

Alvarez turned, gave a stiff little bow to Chen-Lhu. "And you have no objections, Doctor?"

"I've objections, but no authority," Chen-Lhu said. "Is the arm severely injured? I will have my own physicians see to it."

"The arm will recover," Alvarez rumbled.

"He really wants to know if it was actually injured," Martinho said.

Chen-Lhu turned a startled look at Martinho, masked it quickly.

Vierho handed one of the carbines to his chief, said, "Jefe, we have to do this?"

"Why would the good Doctor doubt that my arm was injured?" Alvarez asked.

"He has heard stories," Martinho said.

"What stories?"

"That we bandeirantes don't want to see a good thing end, that we're reinfesting the Green, breeding new insects in secret laboratories."

"That rot!" Alvarez growled.

"Which bandeirantes are supposed to be doing this?" Vierho demanded. He scowled at Chen-Lhu, gripped the carbine as though ready to turn it on the IEO official.

"Easy, Padre," Alvarez said. "The stories never say. It's always *they* or *them*—never names."

Martinho looked toward the place in the lawn where the giant figure of a beetle had disappeared. He found this dalliance with talk far more alluring than the walk across the lawn to that place. The night air carried a sense of lowering menace and . . . hysteria. And the oddest thing of all was the reluctance to take action that could be seen all around him. It was like the lull after a terrible battle in a war.

Well, it is a kind of war, he told himself.

Eight years they'd been fighting this war here in Brazil. The Chinese had taken twenty-two years, but they'd said it could be done here in ten. The thought that it might take twenty-two years here—fourteen more years—momentarily threatened to overwhelm Martinho. He felt a monstrous fatigue.

"You must admit odd things are happening," Chen-Lhu said.

"That we admit," Alvarez said.

"Why does no one suspect the Carsonites?" Vierho asked.

"A good question, Padre," Alvarez said. "They have big support, the Carsonites—all the holdout nations: the US of A, Canada, the United Kingdom, Common Europe."

"All the places where they've never had any real trouble with the insects," Vierho said.

Oddly, it was Chen-Lhu who protested. "No," he said. "The holdout nations don't really care—except that they're happy to see us occupied with this fight."

Martinho nodded. Yes—that was what all the companions of his schooldays in North America had said. They couldn't care less.

"I am going over now and look in that hole," Martinho said.

Alvarez reached out, took Vierho's carbine. He hung it on his good shoulder by the sling, took the control handle of the shield. "I will go with you, Johnny."

Martinho glanced at Vierho, saw the look of terrified relief in the man's face, returned his attention to Alvarez. "Your arm?"

"I still have one good arm. What more do I need?"

"Travis, you stay close behind us," Martinho said.

"My Security men have just arrived," Chen-Lhu said. "Delay a moment and we'll ring that place. I will tell them to bring shields."

"It is wise, Johnny," Alvarez said.

"We will go slowly," Martinho said. "Padre, return to the truck. Tell Ramon to bring it around the Plaza and up onto the edge of the lawn over there. Have the Hermosillo truck direct all its lights onto that place." He nodded ahead of him.

"At once, Jefe."

Vierho headed back for the truck.

"You will not disturb anything there?" Chen-Lhu asked.

"We're as anxious as you to find out what that is," Alvarez said.

"Let's go," Martinho said.

Chen-Lhu trotted off to the right where an IEO field truck could be seen making its way through a side street. The crowd appeared to be giving trouble there, resisting efforts to expel them from the Plaza area.

Alvarez turned the control handle and the shield began crawling across the lawn.

In a low voice, Alvarez said, "Johnny, why doesn't the doctor suspect the Carsonites?"

"He has a spy system as good as anything in the world," Martinho said. "He must know." He kept his gaze on the disturbed patch of lawn ahead of them, that mysterious place beside the fountain.

"But what better way to sabotage us than to discredit the bandeirantes?"

"True, but I don't think Travis Huntington Chen-Lhu would make such a mistake." And he thought: *It is strange how that patch of lawn both attracts and repels.*

"You and I have been rivals at the bid many times, Johnny. Perhaps we forget sometimes that we have a common enemy."

"Do you name that enemy?"

"It's the enemy in the jungles, in the grass of the savannahs and under the ground. The Chinese took twenty-two years . . ."

"Do you suspect them?" Martinho glanced at his companion, noting the glower of concentration of Alvarez's face. "They will not let us inspect their results."

"The Chinese are paranoid. They leaned that way before they ever collided with the Western world and the Western world merely confirmed them in this sickness. Suspect the Chinese? I don't think so."

"I do," Martinho said. "I suspect everyone."

A feeling of gloom overtook him at the sound of his own words. It was true—he suspected everyone, even Benito here, and Chen-Lhu . . . and the lovely Rhin Kelly. He said, "I think often of the ancient insecticides, how the insects grew ever stronger in spite of—or because of—the insect poisons."

A sound behind them caught Martinho's attention. He put a hand on Alvarez's arm, stopped the shield, turned.

It was Vierho followed by a slavecart piled with gear. Martinho identified a long pry bar there, a large body hood that must have been intended for Alvarez, packages of plastic explosive.

"Jefe . . . I thought you would need these things," Vierho said.

A feeling of affection for the Padre swept through Martinho and he spoke bruskly: "Stay close behind and out of the way, you hear?"

"Of course, Jefe. Don't I always?" He held the body hood toward Alvarez. "This I brought for you, Jefe Alvarez, that you might not suffer another hurt."

"I thank you, Padre," Alvarez said, "but I prefer freedom of movement. Besides, this old body has so many scars, one more will make little difference."

Martinho glanced around him, noted that other shields were advancing across the lawn. "Quickly," he said: "we must be the first there."

Alvarez rotated the control handle. Again their shield ground its way toward the fountain.

Vierho came up close beside his chief, spoke in a low voice: "Jefe, there are stories back there at the truck. It is said that some creature ate the pilings from under a warehouse at the waterfront. The warehouse collapsed. People were killed. There is much upset."

"Chen-Lhu hinted at this," Martinho said.

"Is this not the place?" Alvarez asked.

"Stop the shield," Martinho said. He stared at the grass ahead of them, searching out the place—the relationship to the fountain, the grass marked by the previous passage of their shield.

"This is the place," he said. He passed his carbine to Vierho, said, "Give me that prybar ... and a stun charge."

Vierho handed him a small packet of plastic explosive with detonator, the kind of charge they used in the Red areas to break up an insect nest in the ground. Martinho pulled his head shield down tight, took the prybar. "Vierho, cover me from here. Benito—can you use a handlight?"

"Of course, Johnny."

"Jefe ... you are not going to use the shield?"

"There isn't time." He stepped around the shield before Vierho could answer. The beam of a handlight stabbed down at the ground ahead of him. He crouched, slid the tip of the prybar along the grass, digging, pushing. The bar caught, then slipped down into emptiness.

Something touched it down there, and an electric tingle shot all through Martinho.

"Padre, down here," he whispered.

Vierho leaned over him with the carbine. "Jefe?"

"Just ahead of the bar—into the ground."

Vierho aimed, squeezed off two shots.

A violent scrabbling noise erupted under the lawn ahead of them. Something splashed there.

Again, Vierho fired. The blast pellets made a curious thumping sound as they exploded under the ground.

There came the liquid sound of furious activity down there—as though there were a school of fish feeding at the surface.

Silence.

More handlights glared onto the lawn ahead of him. Martinho looked up to see a ring of shields around them—IEO and bandeirante uniforms.

Again he focused on the patch of lawn.

"Padre, I'm going to pry it up. Be ready."

"Of course, Jefe."

Martinho put a foot under the bar as fulcrum, leaned on his end. The trapdoor lifted slowly. It appeared to be sealed with a gummy mixture that came up in trailing sheets. A whiff of sulphur and corrosive sublimate told Martinho what the sealant must be—the butyl carrier he'd fired from the sprayrifle. With a sudden giving, the door swung up, flopped back onto the lawn.

Handlights were beside Martinho now, probing downward to reveal oily black water. It had the smell of the river.

"They came in from the river," Alvarez said.

Chen-Lhu came up beside Martinho, said, "The masqueraders appear to have escaped. How convenient." And he thought: *I was correct to give Rhin her orders when I did. We must get a line into their organization.*

*This is the enemy: this bandeirante leader who was ed-
ucated among the Yankee imperialists. He is one of
those who're trying to destroy us; there can be no other
answer.*

Martinho ignored Chen-Lhu's jibe; he was too weary
even to be angry with the fool. He stood up, looked
around the Plaza. The air held a stillness as though the
entire sky awaited some calamity. A few watchers remained beyond the expanded ring of guards—privi-
leged officials, probably—but the mob had been cleared
back into adjoining streets.

A small red groundcar could be seen coming down
an avenue from the left, its windows glittering under
the slave-lights as it scuttled toward the Plaza. Its three
headlights darted in and out as it skirted people and
vehicles. Guards opened a way for it. Martinho recognized the IEO insignia on its toneau as it neared. The
car jerked to a fast stop at the edge of the lawn and
Rhin Kelly jumped out.

She had changed to coveralls of IEO working green.
They looked almost like sunbleached grass under the
yellow lights of the Plaza.

She strode across the lawn, her attention fixed on
Martinho, thinking: *He must be used and discarded.
He's the enemy. That's obvious now.*

Martinho watched her approach, admiring the grace
and femininity which the simple uniform only accented.

She stopped in front of him, spoke in a husky, urgent
voice: "Senhor Martinho, I've come to save your life."

He shook his head, not quite believing he'd heard her
correctly. "What . . ."

"All hell is about to break loose," she said.

Martinho grew aware of distant shouting.

"A mob," she said. "Armed."

"What the devil's going on?" he demanded.

"There've been some deaths tonight," she said. "Women and children among them. A section of the hill collapsed behind Monte Ochoa. There're burrows all through that hill."

Vierho said, "The orphanage . . ."

"Yes," she said. "The orphanage and convent on Monte Ochoa were buried. Bandeirantes are blamed. You know what is being said about . . ."

"I'll talk to these people," Martinho said. He felt outrage at the thought of being threatened by those he served. "This is nonsense! We've done nothing to . . ."

"Jefe," Vierho said, "you do not reason with a mob."

"Two men of the Lifcado band already have been lynched," Rhin said. "You have a chance if you run now. Your trucks are here, enough for all of you."

Vierho took his arm. "Jefe, we must do as she says."

Martinho stood silently, hearing the information being passed among the bandeirantes around them—"A mob . . . the blame on us . . . orphanage . . ."

"Where could we go?" he asked.

"This violence appears to be local," Chen-Lhu said. He paused, listening: the mob sounds had grown louder. "Go to your father's place in Cuiaba. Take your band with you. The others can go to your bases in the Red."

"Why must I . . ."

"I will send Rhin to you when we've devised a plan of action."

"I must know where to find you," Rhin said, picking up her cue. And she thought: *The father's place, yes. That must be the center of it . . . there or the Goyaz as Travis suspects.*

"But we've done nothing," Martinho said.

"Please," she said.

Vierho tugged his arm.

Martinho took a deep breath. "Padre, go with the

men. It'll be safer out there in the Red. I'll take the small truck and go to Cuiaba. I must discuss this with my father, the Prefect. Someone must get to the seat of government and make the people there listen."

"Listen to what?" Alvarez asked.

"The . . . work must be halted . . . temporarily," Martinho said. "There must be an investigation."

"That is foolish!" Alvarez barked. "Who will listen to such talk as that?"

Martinho tried to swallow in a dry throat. The night around him felt cold, oppressive . . . and the mob sounds had grown louder. Police and military guards wouldn't be able to hold back that angered, many-celled monster much longer.

"They cannot afford to listen," Alvarez muttered. "Even if you're right."

The mob sounds punctuated the truth in those words, Martinho knew. The men in power couldn't admit failure. They were in power because of certain promises. If those promises weren't kept, someone would have to be found to take the blame.

Perhaps someone's already been found, he thought.

He allowed Vierho to lead him then toward the trucks.

4

It was a cave high above wet black rocks of a Goyaz river gorge. In the cave, thoughts pulsed through a brain as it listened to a radio on which a human announcer related the day's news: riots in Bahia, bandeirantes lynched, paratroopers landed to restore order. . . .

The radio, a small battery-powered portable, made a tinny racket in the cave that irritated the brain's sensors, but human news had to be monitored . . . as long as the batteries held out. Perhaps biochemical cells could be used after that, but the brain's mechanical knowledge was limited. Theory it had in abundance from filmbook libraries abandoned in the Red, but practical knowledge was another matter.

There'd been a portable television for awhile, but its range had been limited and now it no longer worked.

News ended and music blared from the speaker. The brain signaled for the instrument to be silenced. The brain lay there then in the welcome silence, thinking, pulsing.

It was a mass about four meters in diameter and half

a meter deep, knowing itself as a "Supreme Integration" filled with passive alertness, yet always more than a little irritated by the necessities which kept it anchored to this cave sanctuary.

A mobile sensory mask which it could shift and flex at will—forming now a disc, then a membranous funnel, and even the simulation of a giant human face—lay like a cap across the brain's surface, its sensors directed toward gray dawnlight at the cave mouth.

The rhythmic pulsing of a yellow sac at one side pumped a dark viscous fluid into the brain. Wingless insects crawled over its surface membranes—inspecting, repairing, giving special foods where needed.

Specialist hives of winged insects clustered in fissures of the cave, some producing acids, some breaking down the acids for their oxygen, some digesting, some providing the muscles for pumping.

A bitter-clean acid smell permeated the cave.

Insects flew in and out of the dawnlight. Some paused to dance and sway and hum for the brain's sensors; some used modulated stridulations to report; some appeared in special groups aligned a special way; some formed complex patterns with changes in coloration; some waved antennae in intricate ways.

Now came the relay from Bahia: "Much rain—wet ground; the burrows of our listening post collapsed. An observer was seen and attacked, but a monitor brought it to safety by tunneling from the river. The river tunnels brought collapse of a structure there. We left no evidence except what was seen of us by the humans. Those of us who could not escape were destroyed.

"There were deaths among the humans."

Deaths among the humans, the brain reflected. *Then the radio reports were correct.*

This was disaster.

The brain's oxygen demand increased; attendant insects sped over it; the pumping rhythm increased its pace.

The humans will believe themselves attacked, the brain thought. *The complex defense posture of humankind will be be activated. To penetrate that posture with calm reasoning will be most difficult if not impossible.*

Who can reason with unreason?

The humans were very difficult to understand with their gods and their accumulation patterns.

"Business" was what the books called their accumulation pattern, but the sense of it eluded the brain. Money could not be eaten, it stored no apparent energy, and was a poor building material. Wattle and daub *taipa* houses of the poorest humans had more substance.

Still, the humans grubbed for it. The stuff had to be important. It had to be every bit as important as their god-concept, which appeared to be something like a supreme integration whose substance and location could not be defined. Most disturbing.

Somewhere, the brain felt, there must be a thought-mode to make these matters understandable, but the pattern escaped it.

The brain thought then how strange it was, this *thought-mode* of existence, this transference of internal energy to create imaginary visions that were in fact plans and schemes and that sometimes must move for a way along non-survival paths. How curious, how subtle, yet how beautiful was this human discovery which had now been copied and adapted to the uses of other creatures. How admirable and elevated it was, this manipulation of the universe that existed only within the passive confines of imagination.

For a moment, the brain tested itself, attempting to simulate human emotions. Fear and the hive-oneness—

these it could understand. But the permutations, the variance of fear called *hate*, the blister-sided reflexes—these were more difficult.

Never once did the brain consider that it once had been part of a human and subject to such emotions. Intrusion of those thoughts had been found irritating. They had been excised at its own direction. Now the brain was only vaguely like its human counterpart, larger, more complex. No human circulatory system could support its needs for nourishment. No merely human sensory system could supply its voracious appetite for information.

It was simply *Brain*, a functional part of the superhive system—more important now than even the queens.

"Which class of humans was killed?" it asked.

The answer came in low stridulations: "Workers, females, immature humans and some barren queens."

Females and immature humans, the brain thought. It formed on the screen of its awareness an Indian curse whose source had been excised. With such deaths, the human reaction would be most violent. Quick action was imperative.

"What word from our messengers who penetrated the barrier?" the brain asked.

The answer came: "Hiding place of the messenger group unknown."

"The messengers must be found. They must stay in hiding until a more opportune moment. Communicate that order at once."

Specialist workers departed at once to obey the order.

"We must capture a more varied sample of humans," the brain commanded. "We must find a vulnerable leader among them. Send out observers and messengers and action units. Report as soon as possible."

The brain listened then, hearing its orders being

obeyed, thinking of the messages being carried off across the distances. Vague frustrations stirred in the brain, needs for which it had no answers. It raised its sensory mask on supporting stalks, formed eyes and focused them upon the cave-mouth.

Full daylight.

Now it could only wait.

Waiting was the most difficult part of existence.

The brain began examining this thought, forming corollaries and interweavings of possible alternatives to the waiting process, imagining projections of physical growth that might obviate waiting.

The thoughts produced a form of intellectual indigestion that alarmed the supporting hives. They buzzed furiously around the brain, shielding it, feeding it, forming phalanxes of warriors in the cavemouth.

This action brought worry to the brain.

The brain knew what had set its cohorts into motion: guarding the *precious-core* of the hive was an instinct rooted in species survival. Primitive hive units could not change that pattern, the brain realized. They had to change, though. They had to learn mobility of need, mobility of judgment, taking each situation as a unique *thing*.

I must go on teaching and learning, the brain thought.

It wished then for reports from the tiny observers it had sent eastward, The need for information from that area was enormous—something to fill out the bits and scraps garnered from the listening posts. Vital proof might come from there to sway humankind from its headlong plunge into the *death-for-all*.

Slowly, the hive reduced its activity as the brain withdrew from the painful edges of thought.

Meanwhile, we wait, the brain told itself.

And it set itself the problem of a slight gene alteration

in a wingless wasp to improve on the oxygen generation system.

Senhor Gabriel Martinho, prefect of the Mato Grosso Barrier Compact, paced his study, muttering to himself as he passed a tall, narrow window that admitted evening sunlight. Occasionally he paused to glare down at his son, Joao, who sat on a tapir-leather sofa beneath one of the bookcases that lined the room.

The elder Martinho was a dark wisp of a man, limb thin, with gray hair and cavernous brown eyes above an eagle nose, slit mouth and boot-toe chin. He wore old style black clothing as befitted his position. His linen gleamed white against the black. Golden cuffstuds glittered as he waved his arms.

"I am an object of ridicule," he snarled.

Joao absorbed the statement in silence. After a full week of listening to his father's outbursts, Joao had learned the value of silence. He looked down at his bandeirante dress whites, the trousers tucked into calf-high jungle boots—everything crisp and glistening and clean while his men sweated out the preliminary survey on the Serra dos Parcecis.

It began to grow dark in the room, quick tropic darkness hurried by thunderheads piled along the horizon. The waning daylight carried a hazed blue cast. Heat lightning spattered the patch of sky visible through the tall window, and sent dazzling electric radiance into the study. Drumming thunder followed. As though that were the signal, the house sensors turned on lights wherever there were humans. Yellow illumination filled the study.

The Prefect stopped in front of his son. "Why does my own son, the renowned Jefe of the Irmandades, spout such Carsonite stupidities?"

Joao looked at the floor between his boots. The fight in the Bahia Plaza, the flight from the mob—all that just a week away—seemed an eternity distant, part of someone else's past. This day had seen a succession of important political people through his father's study— polite greetings for the renowned Joao Martinho and low-voiced conferences with his father.

The old man was fighting for his son—Joao knew this. But the elder Martinho could only fight in the way he knew best: through the ritual kin system, with pistolao "pull"—maneuvering behind the scenes, exchanging power-promises, assembling political strength where it counted. Not once would he consider Joao's suspicions and doubts. The Irmandades, Alvarez and his Hermosillos—anyone who'd had anything to do with the Piratininga—were in bad odor right now. Fences must be mended.

"Stop the realignment?" the old man muttered. "Delay the Marcha para Oeste? Are you mad? How do you think I hold my office? Me! A descendant of fidalgoes whose ancestors ruled one of the original capitanias! We are not bugres whose ancestors were hidden by Rui Barbosa, yet the *caboclos* call me 'Father of the Poor.' I did not gain that name through stupidity."

"Father, if you'd only . . ."

"Be silent! I have our *panelinha*, our little pot, boiling merrily. All will be well."

Joao sighed. He felt both resentment and shame at his position here. The Prefect had been semi-retired until this emergency—a *very* weak heart. Now, to disturb the old man this way . . . but he persisted in being so blind!

"Investigate, you say," the old man mocked him. "Investigate what? Right now we don't want investigation and suspicions. The government, thanks to a week of work by my friends, takes the attitude that everything's normal. They're almost ready to blame the Carsonites for the Bahia tragedy."

"But they have no evidence," Joao said. "You admitted that yourself."

"Evidence is of no importance in such a time," his father said. "All that counts is that we move suspicion far away from ourselves. We must gain time. Besides, this is the very sort of thing the Carsonites might've done."

"But might not've done," Joao said.

It was as though the old man had not heard. "Just last week," he said, gesturing with arm swinging wide, "the day before you arrived here like an insane whirlwind—that very day, I spoke to the Lacuia farmers at the request of my friend the Minister of Agriculture. And do you know that rabble laughed at me! I said we'd increase the Green by ten thousand hectares this month. They laughed. They said: 'Your own son doesn't even believe this!' I see now why they say such things. Stop the march to the west, indeed."

"You've seen the reports from Bahia," Joao said. "The IEO's own investigators . . ."

"The IEO! That sly Chinese whose face tells you nothing. He is more bahiano than the bahianos themselves, that sly one. And this new *female* Doutor he sends everywhere to snoop and pry. His *mae de santo*, his *sidaga*—the stories you hear about that one, I can tell you. Only yesterday, it was said . . ."

"I don't want to hear!"

The old man fell silent, stared down at him. "Ahhhh?"

"Ahhhh!" Joao said. "What does that mean?"

"That means *Ahhhh!*" the old man said.

"She's a very beautiful woman," Joao said.

"So I have heard it reported. And many men have sampled that beauty . . . so it is said."

"I don't believe it!"

"Joao," the Prefect said, "listen to an old man whose experience has given him wisdom. That is a dangerous woman. She is owned body and soul by the IEO, which is an organization that often interferes with our business. You, you are an *empreiteiro*, a contractor of renown, whose abilities and successes are sure to have aroused envy in some quarters. That woman is supposed to be a *Doutor* of the insects, but her actions say she has a *cabide de empregos*. She has a hatstand of jobs. And some of those jobs, ahh, some of those jobs . . ."

"That's enough, Father!"

"As you wish."

"She is supposed to come here soon," Joao said. "I don't want your present attitude to . . ."

"There may be a delay in her visit," the Prefect said.

Joao studied him. "Why?"

"Tuesday last, the day after your little Bahia episode, she was sent to the Goyaz. That very night or the next morning; it is not important."

"Oh?"

"You know what she does in the Goyaz, of course— those stories about a secret bandeirante base there. She is prying into that . . . if she still lives."

Joao's head snapped up. "What?"

"There is a story in the Bahia headquarters of the IEO that she is . . . overdue. An accident, perhaps. It is said that tomorrow the great Travis Huntington Chen-Lhu himself goes to seek his female *Doutor*. What do you think of that?"

"He seemed fond of her, when I saw them in Bahia, but this story about . . ."

"Fond? Oh, yes, indeed."

"You have an evil mind, Father." He took a deep breath. The thought of that lovely woman down somewhere in the deep interland where only jungle creatures now lived, dead or maimed—all that beauty—it left Joao with a feeling of sick emptiness.

"Perhaps you'll wish to march to the west to seek her?"

Joao ignored the jibe, said, "Father, this whole crusade needs a rest period while we find out what's gone wrong."

"If you talked that way in Bahia, I don't blame them for turning on you," the Prefect said. "Perhaps that mob . . ."

"You know what we saw in that Plaza!"

"Nonsense, but yesterday's nonsense. This must stop now. You must do nothing to disturb the equilibrium. I command you!"

"People no longer suspect the bandeirantes," Joao said, bitterness in his voice.

"Some still suspect you, yes. And why not, if what I've heard from your own lips is any sample of the way you talk?"

Joao studied the toes of his boots, the polish glittering black. He found their unmarked surfaces somehow symbolic of his father's life. "I'm sorry I've distressed you, Father," he said. "Sometimes I regret that I'm a bandeirante, but"—he shrugged—"without that, how could I have learned the things I've told you? The truth is . . ."

"Joao!" His father's voice quavered. "Do you sit there and tell me you besmirched our honor? Did you swear a false oath when you formed your Irmandades?"

"That's not the way it was, Father."

"Oh? Then how was it?"

Joao pulled a sprayman's emblem from his breast pocket, fingered it. "I believed it . . . then. We could shape mutated bees to fill every gap in the insect ecology. It was a . . . Great Crusade. This I believed. Like the people of China, I said: 'Only the useful shall live!' And I meant it. But that was quite a few years ago, father. I've come to realize since then that we don't have complete understanding of what's useful."

"It was a mistake to have you educated in North America," his father said. "I blame myself for that. Yes—I am the one to blame for that. There's where you absorbed this Carsonite heresy. It's all well and good for *them* to refuse to join us in the Ecological Realignment; they don't have as many millions of mouths to feed. But my own son!"

Joao spoke defensively: "Out in the Red you see things, father. These things are difficult to explain. Plants look healthier out there. The fruit is . . ."

"A purely temporary condition," his father said. "We'll shape bees to meet whatever need we find. The destroyers take food from our mouths. It's very simple. They must die and be replaced by creatures which serve a function useful to man."

"The birds are dying, Father."

"We're saving the birds! We've specimens of every kind in our sanctuaries. We'll provide new foods for them to . . ."

"Some plants already have disappeared from lack of natural pollination."

"No useful plant has been lost!"

"And what happens," Joao asked, "if our barriers are breached by the insects before we've replaced the population of natural predators? What happens then?"

The elder Martinho shook a thin finger under his son's nose. "This nonsense must stop! I'll hear no more of it! Do you hear?"

"Please calm yourself, Father."

"Calm myself? How can I calm myself in the face of . . . of . . . this? You here hiding like a common criminal! Riots in Bahia and Santarem and . . ."

"Father, stop it!"

"I will not stop it. Do you know what else those mameluco farmers in Lacuia said to me? They said bandeirantes have been seen reinfesting the Green to prolong their jobs! That is what they said."

"That's nonsense, father!"

"Of course it's nonsense! But it's a natural consequence of defeatist talk just such as I've heard from you here today. And all the setbacks we suffer add strength to such charges."

"Setbacks, Father?"

"I have said it: setbacks!"

Senhor Prefect Martinho turned, paced to his desk and back. Again, he stopped in front of his son, placed hands on hips. "You refer, of course, to the Piratininga."

"Among others."

"Your Irmandades were on that line."

"Not so much as a flea got through us!"

"Yet a week ago the Piratininga was Green. Today . . ." He pointed to his desk. "You saw the report. It's crawling. Crawling!"

"I cannot watch every bandeirante in the Mato Grosso," Joao said. "If they . . ."

"The IEO gives us only six months to clean up," the elder Martinho said. He raised his hands, palms up; his face was flushed. "Six months!"

"If you'd only go to your friends in the government and convince them of what . . ."

"Convince them? Walk in and tell them to commit political suicide? My friends? Do you know the IEO is threatening to throw an embargo around all Brazil—the way they've done with North America?" He lowered his hands. "Can you imagine the pressures on us? Can you imagine the things that I must listen to about the bandeirantes and especially about my own son?"

Joao gripped the sprayman's emblem until it dug into his palm. A week of this was almost more than he could bear. He longed to be out with his men, preparing for the fight in the Serra dos Parecis. His father had been too long in politics to change—and Joao realized this with a feeling of sickness. He looked up at his father. If only the old man weren't so excitable—the concern about his heart. "You excite yourself needlessly," he said.

"Excite myself!"

The Prefect's nostrils dilated; he bent toward his son. "Already we've gone past two deadlines—the Piratininga and the Tefe. That is land in there, don't you understand? And there are no men on that land, farming it, making it produce!"

"The Piratininga was not a full barrier, Father. We'd just cleared the . . ."

"Yes! And we gained an extension of deadline when I announced that my son and the redoubtable Benito Alvarez had cleared the Piratininga. How do you explain now that it is reinfested, that we have the work to do over?"

"I don't explain it."

Joao returned the sprayman's emblem to his pocket. It was obvious he wouldn't be able to reason with his father. It had been growing increasingly obvious throughout the week. Frustration sent a nerve quivering along Joao's jaw. The old man had to be convinced, though! Someone had to be convinced. Someone of his father's political stature had to get back to the Bureau, shake them up there and make them listen.

The Prefect returned to his desk, sat down. He picked

up an antique crucifix, one that the great Aleihadinho had carved in ivory. He lifted it, obviously seeking to restore his serenity, but his eyes went wide and glaring. Slowly, he returned the crucifix to his desk, keeping his attention on it.

"Joao," he whispered.

It's his heart! Joao thought.

He leaped to his feet, rushed to his father's side. "Father! What is it?"

The elder Martinho pointed, hand trembling.

Through the spiked crown of thorns, across the agonized ivory face, over the straining muscles of the Christ figure crawled an insect. It was the color of the ivory, shaped faintly like a beetle but with a multi-clawed fringe along wings and thorax, and with furry edgings to its abnormally long antennae.

The elder Martinho reached for a roll of papers to smash the insect, but Joao restrained him with a hand. "Wait. This a new one. I've never seen anything like it. Give me a handlight. We must follow it, find where it nests."

The Prefect muttered under his breath, withdrew a small permalight from a desk drawer, handed the light to his son.

Joao held the light without using it, peered at the insect. "How strange it is," he said. "See how it exactly matches the tones of ivory."

The insect stopped, pointed its antennae toward the men.

"Things have been seen," Joao said. "There are stories. Something like this was found near one of the barrier villages last month. It was inside the Green . . . on a path beside a river. Remember the report? Two farmers found it while searching for a sick man." Joao looked at his father. "They're very watchful for sickness in the newly Green, you know. There've been epidemics . . . and that's another thing."

"There's no relationship," his father snapped. "Without insects to carry diseases, we'll have less illness."

"Perhaps," Joao said, but his tone said he didn't believe it.

Joao returned his attention to the insect on the crucifix. "I don't think our ecologists know all they say they do. And I mistrust our Chinese advisors. They speak in such flowery terms of the benefits from eliminating insect pests, but they won't let us inspect their Green. Excuses. Always excuses. I think they're having troubles they don't wish us to discover."

"That's foolishness," the elder Martinho growled, but his tone said this wasn't a position he cared to defend. "They are honorable men—with a few exceptions I could name. And their way of life is closer to our socialism than it is to the decadent capitalism of North America. Your trouble is you see them too much through the eyes of those who educated you."

"I'll wager this insect's one of the spontaneous mutations," Joao said. "It's almost as though they appeared by some plan. . . . Find me something in which to capture this creature and take it to the lab."

The elder Martinho remained standing beside his chair. "Where'll you say it was found?"

"Right here."

"You would not hesitate to expose us to more ridicule, is that it?"

"But Father . . ."

"Can't you hear what they'll say? In his own home this insect is found. It's a strange new kind. Perhaps he breeds them there to reinfest the Green."

"Now, *you're* talking nonsense, Father. Mutations are common in a threatened species. And we can't deny there's threat to these insects—the poisons, the barrier vibrations, the traps. Get me that container, Father. I can't leave this creature, or I'd get the container myself."

"And you will tell where it was found?"

"I can do nothing else! We must cordon off this entire area, search out the nests. This could be . . . an accident, of course, but . . ."

"Or a deliberate attempt to embarrass me."

Joao looked up, studied his father. *That* was a possibility, of course. His father did have enemies. And the Carsonites were always there to be considered. They had friends in many places . . . and some were fanatics who'd stoop to any scheme. Still . . .

Decision came to Joao. He returned his attention to the motionless insect. His father had to be convinced, and here was the perfect lever for the argument.

"Look at this creature, Father," he said.

The Prefect turned a reluctant gaze on the insect.

"Our earliest poisons," Joao said, "killed off the weak and selected out those immune to this threat from humans. Only the immune remained to breed. The poisons we use now—some of them—don't leave such loopholes . . . and the deadly vibrations at the barriers . . ." He shrugged. "Still, this is a form of beetle, Father, and somehow it got through the barriers. I'll show you a thing."

Joao drew a long, thin whistle of shiny metal from his breast pocket. "There was a time when this called countless beetles to their deaths. I merely had to tune it across their attraction spectrum." He put the whistle to his lips, blew into it, all the while turning the end of it.

No sound audible to human ears emerged from the instrument, but the beetle's antennae writhed.

Joao removed the whistle from his mouth.

The antennae stopped writhing.

"It stayed put, you see," Joao said. "It's a beetle and should be attracted by this whistle, but it did not move. And I think, Father, that there're indications of malignant intelligence among these creatures. They're far from extinction, Father . . . and I believe they're beginning to strike back."

"Malignant intelligence, pah!" his father said.

"You must believe me, Father," Joao said. "No one listens when we bandeirantes report what we've seen. They laugh and say we are too long in the jungle. And where's our evidence? They say such stories could be expected from ignorant farmers . . . then they begin to doubt and suspect us."

"With good reason, I say."

"You will not believe your own son?"

"What has my son said that I can believe?" The elder Martinho was totally the Prefect now, standing erect, glaring coldly at Joao.

"In the Goyaz last month," Joao said, "Antonil Lisboa's bandeirante lost three men who . . ."

"Accidents."

"They were killed with formic acid and oil of copahu."

"They were careless with their poisons. Men grow careless when they . . ."

"No! The formic acid was particularly strong, a heavy concentrate, and identical to that of insect origin. The men were drenched with it."

"You imply that insects such as this . . ." The Prefect pointed to the motionless creature on the crucifix. "That blind creatures such as this . . ."

"They're not blind."

"I did not mean literally blind, but without intelligence," the Prefect said. "You cannot seriously imply that such creatures attacked humans and killed them."

"We've yet to determine precisely how the men were slain," Joao said. "We've only the bodies and physical evidence at the scene. But there've been other deaths, Father, and men missing, and reports of strange creatures that attack bandeirantes. We grow more certain with each day that . . ."

He fell silent as the beetle crawled off the crucifix onto the desk. Immediately it darkened to brown, blended with the wood surface.

"Please, Father—get me a container."

The beetle reached the edge of the desk, hesitated. Its antennae curled back, then forward.

"I'll get your container only if you promise to use discretion in your report of where this creature was found," the Prefect said.

"Father, I . . ."

The beetle leaped off the desk far out into the middle of the room, scurried toward the wall, up the wall and into a crack beside the window.

Joao pressed the handlight's switch, directed the beam into the hole which had swallowed the insect. He crossed the room, examined the hole.

"How long has this hole been here, Father?"

"For years. It was a flaw in the masonry . . . an earthquake several years before your mother died, I believe."

Joao crossed to the door in four strides, went through an arched hallway, down a flight of stone steps, through another door and short hall, through a grillwork gate and into the outside garden. He set the handlight at full intensity, washed its blue glare over the wall beneath the study window.

"Joao, what are you doing?"

"My job, Father." Joao glanced back, saw that the

Prefect had followed and stopped just outside the garden gate.

Joao returned his attention to the study wall, washed the glare of light onto the stones beneath the window. He crouched low, running the light along the ground, peered behind each clod, erased all shadows.

The searching scrutiny passed over the raw earth, turned to the bushes, then the lawn.

Joao heard his father come up behind.

"Do you see it?"

"No."

"You should've allowed me to crush it."

Joao stood up, stared upward toward the tiled roof and the eaves. It was full dark all around now, with only the light from the study plus his handlight to reveal details.

A piercing stridulation, almost painful to the ears, filled the air all around them. It came from the outer garden that bordered the road and the stone fence. Even after it was gone, the sound seemed to hang all around them. It made Joao think of the hunting cry of jungle predators. A shiver moved up his spine. He turned toward the driveway where he had parked his airtruck, sent the handlight stabbing there.

"What a strange sound," his father said. "I . . ." He broke off, stared at the lawn. "What is that?"

The lawn appeared to be in motion, reaching out toward them like a wave curling on a beach. Already the wave had cut them off from the entrance to the house. It still was some ten paces away, but moving in rapidly.

Joao clutched his father's arm. He spoke quietly, hoping not to alarm the old man further, mindful of the weak heart. "We must get to my truck, Father. We must run across them."

"Them?"

"Those are like the insect we saw inside, Father—millions of them. They are attacking. Perhaps they're not beetles after all. Perhaps they're like army ants. We must make it to the truck. I have equipment and supplies there to fight them off. We'll be safe in the truck. It's a bandeirante truck, Father. You must run with me, do you understand? I'll help you, but you must not stumble and fall into them."

"I understand."

They began to run, Joao holding his father's arm, pointing the way with the light.

Let his heart be strong enough, Joao prayed.

They were into the wave of insects then, but the creatures leaped aside, opening a path which closed behind the running men.

The white form of the airtruck loomed out of the shadows at the far curve of the driveway about fifteen meters ahead.

"Joao . . . my heart," the elder Martinho gasped.

"You can make it," Joao panted. "Faster!" He almost lifted his father from the ground for the last few paces.

They were at the wide rear doors into the truck's lab compartment now. Joao yanked open the doors, slapped the light switch on the left wall, reached for a hood and sprayrifle. He stopped, stared into the yellow-lighted interior.

Two men sat there—*sertao* Indians, by the look of them, with bright glaring eyes and bang-cut black hair beneath straw hats. They looked to be identical twins, even to the same mud-gray clothing and sandals, leather shoulder bags. The beetle-like insects crawled around them, up the lab walls, over the instruments and vials.

"What the devil?" Joao blurted.

One of the pair lifted a qena flute, gestured with it.

He spoke in a rasping, oddly inflected voice: "Enter. You will not be harmed if you obey."

Joao felt his father sag, caught the old man in his arms. How light he felt. The old man breathed in short, painful gasps. His face was a pale blue. Sweat stood out on his forehead.

"Joao," the Prefect whispered. "Pain . . . my chest."

"The medicine," Joao said. "Where is your medicine?"

"House," the old man said. "Desk."

"It appears to be dying," one of the Indians rasped.

Still holding his father in his arms, Joao whirled toward the pair, blazed: "I don't know who you are or why you loosed those bugs here, but my father's dying and needs help. Get out of my way!"

"Obey or both die," said the Indian with the flute. "Enter."

"He needs his medicine and a doctor," Joao pleaded. He didn't like the way the Indian pointed that flute. The motion suggested the instrument was actually a weapon.

"What part has failed?" asked the other Indian. He stared curiously at Joao's father. The old man's breathing had become shallow and rapid.

"It's his heart," Joao said. "I know you farmers don't think he's acted fast enough for . . ."

"Not farmers," said the one with the flute. "Heart?"

"Pump," said the other.

"Pump," said the Indian with the flute. He stood up from the bench at the front of the lab, gestured down. "Put . . . father here."

The other one got off the bench, stood aside.

In spite of fear for his father, Joao was caught by the strange appearance of this pair, the fine, scale-like lines in their skin, the glittering brilliance of their eyes. Were they hopped up on some jungle narcotic?

"Put father here," repeated the one with the flute. Again, he pointed at the bench. "Help can be . . ."

"Attained," said the other one.

"Attained," said the one with the flute.

Joao focused now the masses of insects around the walls, the waiting quietude in their ranks. They *were* like the one in the study. Identical.

The old man's breathing now was very shallow, very rapid. Joao felt the fluttering of each breath in his arms and against his chest.

He's dying, Joao thought in desperation.

"Help can be attained," repeated the Indian with the flute. "If you obey, we will not harm."

The Indian lifted his flute, pointed it at Joao. "Obey."

There was no mistaking the gesture. The thing was a weapon.

Slowly, Joao stepped up into the truck, crossed to the bench, lowered his father gently onto the padded surface.

The Indian with the flute motioned him to step back and he obeyed.

The other Indian bent over the elder Martinho's head, raised an eyelid. There was a professional directness about the gesture that startled Joao. The Indian pushed gently on the dying man's diaphragm, removed the Prefect's belt, loosened his collar. A stubby brown finger was placed against the artery in the old man's neck.

"Very weak," the Indian rasped.

Joao took another look at the Indian, wondering at a *sertao* backwoodsman who behaved like a doctor.

"Hospital," the Indian agreed.

"Hospital?" asked the one with the flute.

A low, stridulant hissing came from the other Indian.

"Hospital," said the one with the flute.

That stridulant hissing! Joao stared at the Indian beside the Prefect. That sound had been reminiscent of the call that had echoed across the lawn.

The one with the flute poked him, said, "You. Go into front and maneuver this . . ."

"Vehicle," said the one beside Joao's father.

"Vehicle," said the one with the flute.

"Hospital?" Joao pleaded.

"Hospital," agreed the one with the flute.

Once more, Joao looked at his father. The old man was so still. The other Indian already was strapping the elder Martinho to the bench in preparation for flight. How competent the man appeared in spite of his backwoods look.

"Obey," said the one with the flute.

Joao opened the hatch into the front compartment, slipped through, felt the armed Indian follow. A few drops of rain spattered darkly against the curved windshield. Joao squeezed into the operator's seat. The compartment went dark as the hatch was closed. Solenoids threw the automatic hatch dogs with a dull thump. Joao turned on the dash standby lights, noted how the Indian crouched behind him, flute pointed and ready.

A dart gun of some kind, Joao guessed. *Probably poison.*

He punched the igniter button on the dash, strapped himself in while waiting for the turbines to build up speed. The Indian still crouched behind him without safety harness—vulnerable now if the airtruck were spun sharply.

Joao flicked the communications switch on the lower left corner of the dash, looked into the tiny screen there giving him a view of the lab compartment. The rear doors were open. He closed them by hydraulic remote. His father lay securely strapped to the bench, the other Indian seated at his head.

The turbines reached their whining peak.

Joao switched on the lights, engaged hydrostatic drive. The truck lifted about ten centimeters, angled upward as Joao increased pump displacement. He turned left onto the street, lifted another two meters to increase speed, headed toward the lights of a boulevard.

The Indian spoke beside his ear: "Turn toward the mountain over there." A hand came forward, pointed to the right.

The Alejandro Clinic is in the foothills, Joao thought. *Yes, that's the correct direction.*

Joao made the indicated turn down a cross street that angled toward the boulevard.

Casually, he gave pump displacement another boost, lifted another meter and increased speed once more. In the same motion, he switched on the intercom to the rear compartment, keyed it for the amplifier and pickup beneath the bench where his father lay.

The pickup, capable of making a dropped pin sound like cannon, emitted only a distant hissing and rasping. Joao increased amplification. The instrument should have been transmitting the old man's heartbeats now, sending a noticeable drum-thump into the forward cabin.

There was no sound but that hissing, rasping.

Tears blurred Joao's eyes. He shook his head to clear them.

My father's dead, he thought. *Killed by these crazy backwoodsmen.*

He noted in the dash screen that the Indian back there had a hand under the elder Martinho's back. The Indian appeared to be massaging the dead man's back. The rhythmic rasping matched the motion.

Anger filled Joao. He felt like diving the airtruck into anabutment, dying himself to kill these crazy men.

The truck was approaching the city's outskirts. Ring-girders circled off to the left, giving access to the boulevard. This was an area of small gardens and cottages protected by overfly canopies.

Joao lifted the airtruck over the canopies, headed toward the boulevard. *To the clinic, yes*, he thought. *But it's too late*.

In that instant, he realized there were no heartbeats at all coming from the rear compartment—only that slow, rhythmic grating plus, now that his ears searched for it, a cicada-like hum up and down the scale.

"To the mountains, there," said the Indian behind him. Again that hand came forward to point off to the right.

Joao, with the hand close to his eyes illuminated by the dash lights, saw the scale-like parts of a finger shift position. In that shift, he recognized the scale shapes by their claw fringes.

The beetles!

*The finger was composed of linked beetles working in uni*son!

Joao turned; stared into the Indian's eyes, saw then why they glistened so brightly: they were composed of thousands of tiny facets.

"Hospital, there," the creature beside him said, pointing.

Joao turned back to the controls, fought to keep from losing composure. They weren't Indians . . . they weren't even humans. They were insects—some kind of hive-cluster shaped and organized to mimic a man.

The implications of this discovery raced through his mind. How did they support their weight? How did they feed and breathe?

How did they speak?

Every personal concern had to be subordinated to the

urgent need for getting this information and proof of it back to one of the big government labs where the facts could be explored.

Even the death of his father could not be considered now. Joao knew he had to capture one of these things, get out with it. He reached overhead, flicked on the command transmitter, set its beacon for a homing call. *Let some of my Irmaos be awake and monitoring their sets,* he prayed.

"More to the right," rasped the creature behind him.

Again Joao corrected course.

The voice—that rasping, stridulant sound. Again, Joao asked himself how the creature could produce that simulation of human speech. The coordination required for that action had profound implications.

Joao looked out to his left. The moon was high overhead now, illuminating a line of bandeirante towers off there. The first barrier.

The truck would be out of the Green soon and into the Gray of the poorest Resettlement Plan farms—then, beyond that, another barrier and the Great Red that stretched in reaching fingers through the Goyaz and the inner Mato Grosso, far out to the Andes where teams were coming down from Ecuador. Joao could see scattered lights of Resettlement Plan farms ahead, darkness beyond.

The airtruck was going faster than he wanted, but Joao knew he dared not slow it. They might become suspicious.

"You must go higher," said the creature behind him.

Joao increased pump displacement, raised the nose. He leveled off at three hundred meters.

More bandeirante towers loomed ahead, spaced at closer intervals. Joao picked up the barrier signals on his dash meters, looked back at his guard. The dissembler vibrations of the barrier seemed to have no effect on the creature.

Joao looked out his side window and down as they passed over the barrier. No one down there would challenge him, he knew. This was a bandeirante airtruck headed *into* the Red . . . and with its transmitter sending out a homing call. The men down there would assume he was a band leader headed out on contract after a successful bid, calling his men to him for the job. If the barrier guards recognized his call wave, that would only confirm the thought.

Joao Martinho had just completed a successful bid on the serra dos Parecis. All the bandeirantes knew that.

Joao sighed. He could see the moon-silvered snake of the sao Francisco winding off to his left, and the lesser waterways like threads raveled out of the foothills.

I must find the nest—wherever we're headed, Joao thought.

He wondered if he dared turn on his receiver—but if his men started reporting in . . . No. That would make the creatures suspect; they might take violent counteraction.

My men will realize something's wrong when I don't answer, he thought. *They'll follow.*

If any of them hear my call.

"How far are we going?" Joao asked.

"Very far," the guard said.

Joao settled himself for a long trip. *I must be patient*, he thought. *I must be as patient as a spider waiting beside her web.*

Hours droned past: two, three . . . four.

Nothing but moonlighted jungle sped beneath the truck, and the moon lay low on the horizon, near setting. This was the deep Red where broadcast poisons had been used at first with near disastrous results. This was

welcome to the
Downingtown office

C034

Cable

4:16pm 3-10-07 0000

where the first wild mutations had been discovered.

The Goyaz.

This is where my father said Rhin Kelly went, Joao thought. *Is she down there now?*

The moonfrosted jungle told him nothing.

The Goyaz: this was the region being saved for the final assault, using mobile barrier lines when the circle was short enough.

"How much farther?" Joao asked.

"Soon."

Joao armed the emergency charge that would separate the front and rear compartments of the truck when he fired it. The stub wings of the front pod and its emergency rocket motors would get him back into bandeirante country.

With the *specimen* behind him safely subdued, Joao hoped.

He looked up through the canopy, scanned the horizon as far as he could. Was that moonlight glistening on a truck far back to the right? He couldn't be certain . . . but it seemed to be.

"Soon?" Joao asked.

"Ahead," the creature rasped.

The modulated stridulation beneath that voice sent a shiver along Joao's spine. Joao said, "My father . . ."

"Hospital for . . . the father . . . ahead," the creature said.

It would be dawn soon, Joao realized. He could see the first false line of light along the horizon behind. This night had passed so swiftly. Joao wondered if his guard had injected some time-distorting drug into him without his knowledge. He thought not. He felt alert, maintaining himself in the necessities of each moment. There wasn't time for fatigue or boredom when he had to record every landmark half-visible in the night, sense

everything he could about these creatures around him.
The bitter-clean smell of oxalic acid hinted at acid-to-
oxygen chemistry.

But how did they coordinate all those separate insect
units?

They appeared conscious. Was that more mimicry?
What did they use for a brain?

Dawn came, revealing the plateau of the Mato
Grosso: a caldron of liquid green boiling over the edge
of the world. Joao looked out his side windows in time
to see the truck's long shadow bounce across a clearing:
stark galvanized metal roofs against the green—a *si-
tiante* abandoned in the Resettlement, or perhaps the
barracao of a *fazenda* on the coffee frontier. It had been
a likely place for a warehouse, standing as it had beside
a small stream with the land around it bearing signs of
riverbank agriculture.

Joao knew this region; he could put the bandeirante
grid map over it in his imagination—five degrees of
latitude and six degrees of longitude it covered. Once
it had been a place of isolated fazendas farmed by independent browns and blacks and *branco sertanistos*
chained to the encomendero plantation system. The par-
ents of Benito Alvarez had come from here. It was hardwood jungles, narrow rivers with banks overgrown by
lush trees and ferns, savannahs and tangled life.

Here and there along the higher reaches of the rivers
lay the remains of hydroelectric plants long since abandoned, like the one at Paulo Afonso Falls—all replaced
by sun power and atomics.

This was it: the *sertao* of the Goyaz. Even in this age
it remained primitive, a fact blamed on the insects and
disease. It lay there, the last stronghold of teeming insect life in the Western Hemisphere, waiting for a mod-

ern tropical technology to lift it into the Twenty-first Century.

Supplies for the bandeirante assault would come by way of Sao Paulo, by air and by transport on the multi-decked highways, then on antique diesel trains to Itapira, by *aviadores* river runners to Bahus and by airtruck to Registo and Leopoldina on the Araguaya.

And when it was done—the people would return, coming back from the Resettlement Plan areas and the metropolitan shanty towns.

A passage of turbulent air shook the truck, breaking Joao from his reverie, forcing him into an acute consciousness of his situation.

A glance at his guard showed the creature still crouched there, watchful . . . as patient as the Indio it mimicked. The presence of the *thing* behind him had become cumulative, and Joao found himself required to combat a growing sense of revulsion.

The gleaming mechanical pragmatism of the truck pod around him felt as though it were at war with the insect creature. It had no business here in this cabin flying smoothly above the area where its kind ruled supreme.

Joao looked out and down at the green flow of forest, the *zona da mata*. He knew the area beneath him crawled with insects: wire worms in the roots of savannahs, grubs digging in the moist black earth, hopping beetles, dart-like angita wasps, chalcis flies sacred to the still thriving backwoods Xango cult, chiggers, sphecidae, braconidae, fierce hornets, white termites, hemipteric crawlers, blood roaches, thrips, ants, lice, mosquitoes, mites, moths, exotic butterflies, mantidae—and countless unnatural mutations of them all.

That, for sure.

This would be an expensive fight—unless it had already been lost.

I mustn't think that way, Joao told himself. *Out of respect for my father. I mustn't think that way . . . not yet.*

IEO maps showed this region in varied intensities of red. Around the red ran a ring of gray with pink shading where one or two persistent forms of insect life resisted man's poisons, jelly flames, astringents, sonitoxics—the combination of flamant couroq and supersonics that drove insects from their hiding places into waiting death—and all the mechanical traps and luring baits in the bandeirante arsenal.

A grid map would be placed over this area and each thousand-hectare square offered for bid to the independent bands to deinfest.

We bandeirantes are a kind of ultimate predator, Joao thought. *It's no wonder these creatures mimic us.*

But how good, really, was this mimicry? he asked himself. And how deadly to the predators? How far had this gone?

"There," said the creature behind him. The multi-part hand came forward to point toward a black scarp visible ahead of them in the gray light of morning. Heavy mist against the scarp told of a river nearby hidden by the jungle.

This is all I need, Joao thought. *I can find this place again easily.*

His foot kicked the trigger on the floor, releasing a great cloud of orange dye-fog beneath the truck to mark the ground and forest for more than a kilometer around. As he kicked the trigger, Joao began counting down silently the five-second delay to the automatic firing of the separation charge.

It came in a roaring blast that Joao knew would smear

the creature behind against the rear bulkhead. He sent the stub wings out, fed power to the rocket motors and banked hard left. Now he could see the detached rear compartment settling slowly earthward above the dye cloud, its fall cushioned as the pumps of the hydrostatic drive automatically compensated.

I will come back, Father, Joao thought. *You will be buried among family and friends.*

He locked his pod controls, turned to deal with his guard.

A gasp escaped Joao's lips.

The rear bulkhead crawled with insects clustered around something yellow-white and pulsing. The mud-gray shirt and trousers were torn, but insects already were repairing it, spinning out fibers that meshed and sealed on contact. There was a dark yellow sac-like object extruding near the pulsing surface—and glimpses through the insects of a brown skeleton with familiar articulation.

It looked like a human skeleton—but dark and chitinous.

Before his eyes, the thing was reassembling itself— long furry antennae burrowing inward and interlocking, one insect to another, claw fringes weaving together.

The flute weapon wasn't visible, and the thing's leather pouch had been hurled into a rear corner by the blast, but its eyes were in place in their brown sockets, staring at him. The mouth was reforming.

The dark yellow sac contracted, and a voice issued from the half-formed mouth.

"You must listen," it rasped.

Joao gulped, whirled back to the controls, unlocked them and sent the pod into a wild, spinning turn.

A high-pitched rattling buzz sounded behind him. The noise seemed to pick up every bone in his body and shake it. Something crawled on his neck. He slapped it, felt it squash.

All Joao could think of then was escape. He stared out frantically at the earth beneath, glimpsing a blotch of white in a savannah off to his right and in the same instant recognizing another airtruck banking beside him, the insignia of his own Irmandades bright on its side.

The white blotch in the savannah resolved itself into a cluster of tents with an IEO orange and green banner flying beside them. Beyond the flat grass could be seen the curve of a river.

Joao dove for the tents.

Something stung his cheek. Crawling things were in his hair—biting, stinging. He kicked on the braking rockets, aimed for open ground beside the tents. Insects were all over the inside of the pod's glass now, blocking his vision. Joao said a silent prayer, hauled back on the control arm, felt the pod mush out, touch ground, skidding and slewing. He kicked the canopy release before the motion stopped, broke the seal on his safety harness and launched himself up and out to land sprawling on hard ground.

He rolled over and over, eyes tightly closed, feeling the insect bites like fire needles over every exposed part of his body. Hands grabbed him and he felt a jelly hood splash across his face to protect it. Hard spray slammed against him from all sides.

Somewhere in a hood-blurred distance he heard a voice that sounded like Vierho's shout, "Run! This way—run!"

He heard a spraygun fire: *Whoosh!*

And again.

And again.

Hands rolled him over. Spray hit his back. A wash that smelled like neutralizer splashed over him.

An odd thudding sound shook the ground and a voice said, "Mother of God! Would you look at that!"

5

Joao sat up, clawed the jelly hood from his face, stared across the savannah. The grass there seethed and boiled with insects around an Irmandades airtruck.

A voice said, "Did you kill everything inside the pod?"

"Everything that moved." The reply was husky, halting, as though overcoming pain.

"Is there anything in it we can use?"

"The radio's destroyed."

"Of course. That's the first thing they go for."

Joao looked around him, counted seven of his Irmandades—Vierho, Thome, Ramon, Pietr, Lon . . .

His eye was caught by the group clustered beyond his men—Rhin Kelly among them. Her red hair was awry. Dirt streaked her face. There was a wild, glazed look in her green eyes. She was glaring at him.

He saw his pod then, to the right, on its side and just within what appeared to be a perimeter ditch. Foam and spray residue were all over it. His eye traversed the line of the ditch, saw that it ringed a hard-packed dirt area with the tents in the center and savannah beyond. Two men in green IEO uniforms stood beside him holding sprayer handtanks.

Joao returned his attention to Rhin, remembering her as he'd seen her in Bahia's *A'Chigua*. Now she wore a plain IEO field uniform, its green blotched by red-brown dirt. Her eyes held no invitation at all.

"I see poetic justice in this—traitors," she said.

Her hysterical tone of voice caught Joao's ear and it took a second for her words to filter through. *Traitors?*

He grew aware of the bedraggled, worn look of the IEO people.

Vierho approached, helped Joao to his feet, proffered a cloth to wipe off the jelly.

"Jefe, what is happening?" Vierho asked. "We picked up your signal, but you didn't answer."

"Later," Joao rasped as he recognized the anger in Rhin and her companions. Rhin appeared feverish and ill.

Hands brushed Joao, clearing dead insects off him. The pain from the stings and bites receded under the medicant neutralizer.

"Whose skeleton is that in your pod?" one of the IEO people asked.

Before Joao could answer, Rhin said, "Death and skeletons should be nothing new for Joao Martinho, traitor of the Piratininga!"

"They are crazy, that is the only thing, I think," Vierho said.

"Your pets turned on you, didn't they?" Rhin demanded. "The skeleton, that's all that's left of one of you, eh?"

"What is this talk of skeletons?" Vierho asked.

"Your jefe knows," Rhin said.

"Would you be so kind as to explain?" Joao asked.

"I don't need to explain," she said. "Let your friends out there explain." She pointed toward the rim of jungle beyond the savannah.

Joao looked there, saw a line of men in bandeirante white standing untouched amidst the leaping, boiling insects in the jungle shadow. He took a pair of binoculars from around the neck of one of his men, focused on the figures.

Knowing what to look for made the identification easy.

"Padre," Joao said.

Vierho bent close, rubbing at an insect sting beneath the acid scar on his cheek.

In a low voice, Joao explained about the figures at the jungle edge, handed over the glasses so that Vierho could see for himself the fine lines in the skin, the facet-glitter of the eyes.

"Aiee," Vierho said.

"Do you recognize your friends?" Rhin demanded.

Joao ignored her.

Vierho passed along the glasses with an explanation to another of the Irmandades. The two IEO men who had sprayed Joao came close, listening, turned their attention to the figures in the jungle shadows.

One of the IEO men crossed himself.

"That perimeter ditch," Joao said. "What's in it?"

"Couroq jelly," said the IEO man who'd crossed himself. "It's all we had left for an insect barrier."

"That won't stop them," Joao said.

"But it *has* stopped them," the man said.

Joao nodded. He was having unpleasant suspicions about their position here. He looked at Rhin. "Dr. Kelly, where are the rest of your people?" Joao passed his gaze around the IEO personnel, counting. "Surely there're more than six in an IEO field crew."

Her lips compressed, but she remained silent.

The more Joao looked at her, the more ill she appeared.

"So?" Joao said. He glanced around at the tents, seeing their weathered condition. "And where is your equipment, your trucks, lab hut, jitneys?"

"Funny thing you should ask," she said, but there was uncertainty in the sneering quality of her voice—and that definite hysterical undertone. "About a kilometer into the trees over there"—she nodded to her left—"is a wrecked jungle truck containing most of our . . . equipment, as you call it. The track spools of our truck were eaten away by acid before we knew anything was wrong. The lift rotors were destroyed the same way—everything."

"Acid?"

"It smelled like oxalic, but acted more like hydrochloric," said one of her companions, a blond Nordic with a recent acid burn beneath his right eye.

"Start from the beginning," Joao said.

"We were cut off here . . ." He broke off, glanced around.

"Eight days ago," Rhin said.

"Yes," the blond man said. "They got our radio, our truck—they looked like giant chiggers. They can shoot an acid spray about fifteen meters."

"Like the one we saw in the Bahia Plaza?" Joao asked.

"There're three dead specimens in containers in my lab tent," Rhin said. "They're cooperative organization, hive-clusters. See for yourself."

Joao pursed his lips, thinking.

"I heard part of what you told your men there," she said. "D'you expect us to believe that?"

"It's of no importance to me what you believe," Joao said. "How'd you get here?"

"We fought our way in here from the truck using *caramuru* cold-fire spray," said the blond man. "That stalled them a bit. We dragged along what supplies we could, dug a trench around our perimeter, poured in the couroq powder, added the jell and topped it off with all our *copahu* oil . . . and here we sat."

"How many of you?" Joao asked.

"There were fourteen of us in the truck," Rhin said. She stared at Joao, studying him. His manner, his questions—everything consistent with innocence. She tried to reason from this assumption, but her mind bogged down. She wasn't thinking clearly and knew it. Ever since the first attack; there'd been something, a drug very likely, in the stings of the insects that had got through the *caramuru*. But her lab wasn't equipped to determine what the drug was.

Joao rubbed the back of his neck where the insect stings were beginning to burn. He glanced around at his men, assessing their condition and equipment, counted four sprayrifles, saw that the men carried spare charge cylinders on slings around their necks.

And there was his truck pod safe inside the perimeter. The spray they'd poured into it probably had played hob with the control circuits, though. But there still remained the big truck out in the savannah.

"We'd better try to fight our way out to the truck," he said.

"Your truck?" Rhin asked. She looked out to the savannah. "I think it's been too late for that since a few seconds after it landed, bandeirante." She laughed, and the hysteria was close to the surface. "I think in a day or so there'll be a few less traitors. You're caught in your own trap."

Joao whirled to stare at the Irmandade airtruck. It was beginning to tip crazily over onto its left side. "Padre!" he barked. "Tommy! Vince! Get . . ." He broke off as the truck sagged over even farther.

"It's only fair to warn you," Rhin said, "to stay away from the edge of the ditch unless you first spray the opposite side. They can shoot that acid stream at least fifteen meters . . . and as you can see"—she nodded toward the airtruck—"the acid eats metal and even plastic."

"You're insane," Joao said. "Why didn't you warn us immediately? We could've . . ."

"Warn you?"

Her blond companion said, "Dr. Kelly, perhaps we'd . . ."

"Be quiet, Hogar," she said. She glared at the man. "Isn't it time you looked in on Doctor Chen-Lhu?"

"Travis? Is he here?" Joao asked.

"He arrived yesterday with one companion, since deceased," she said. "They were searching for us. Unluckily, they found us. Dr. Chen-Lhu probably will not live through this night." She glared at her Nordic companion. "Hogar!"

"Yes, ma'am," the man said. He shrugged, headed for the tents.

"We lost eight men to your playmates, bandeirante," Rhin said. She looked at the small group of Irmandades. "Our lives are little enough to pay now for the extinction of eight of you . . . traitors!"

"You *are* insane," Joao said, and he felt the beginnings of a crazy anger in himself. Chen-Lhu here . . . dying? That could wait. First there was work to do.

"Stop playing innocent, bandeirante," Rhin said. "We've seen your companions out there. We've seen the new *playmates* you bred . . . and we understand that you were too greedy; your game has gotten out of hand."

"You've not seen my Irmaos doing these things," Joao said. He looked at Thome. "Tommy, keep an eye on these insane ones. Don't permit them to interfere with us." He lifted a sprayrifle and spare charges from one of his men, indicated the other three armed men. "You—come with me."

"Jefe, what do you do?" Vierho asked.

"Salvage what we can from the truck," Joao said.

Vierho sighed, took one of the sprayrifles and charges, motioned their owner to stay with Thome.

"Sure, go get yourselves killed," Rhin said. "Don't think we'll interfere with that!"

Joao stopped himself from turning on her with a burst of outraged curses. His head ached with the anger and the need to suppress it. Presently he walked toward the ditch nearest the stranded airtruck, laid down a hard mist of foamal in the grass beyond, beckoned the others to follow and leaped the ditch.

Later, Joao did not like to think about that time in the savannah. They were out little more than twenty minutes before retreating to the island of tents. Joao and his three companions were acid burned, Vierho and Lon seriously. And they'd salvaged less than an eighth of the material in the truck—mostly food. The salvage did not include a transmitter.

The attack came from all sides, from creatures hidden in the tall grass. Foamal immobilized them temporarily. None of the sprayrifle poisons seemed to do more than slow the creatures. The attack stopped only when the men were safely back behind the ditch.

"It's evident the devils went first for our communications equipment," Vierho gasped. "How could they know?"

"I don't want to guess," Joao said. "Stand still while I treat those burns." Vierho's cheek and shoulder were badly splashed with acid, his clothing peeling away in smoking tatters.

Joao spread neutralizer salve over the area, turned to Lon. The man already was losing flesh off his back, but he stood there panting, waiting.

Rhin came up to help with the treatment and bandaging, but refused to speak, even to answering the simplest questions.

"Do you have any more of this salve?"

Silence.

"Have you taken any samples of the acids?"

Silence.

"How was Chen-Lhu injured?"

Silence.

Presently, Joao touched up three splash burns on his left arm, neutralized the acid and covered the injuries with flesh-tape. He gritted his teeth against the pain, stared at Rhin. "Where are these chigua specimens you killed?"

Silence.

"You are a blind, unprincipled megalomaniac," Joao said, speaking in an even tone. "Don't push me too far."

Her face went pale, and the green eyes blazed, but her lips remained closed.

Joao's arm throbbed, his head ached and he felt there was something vaguely wrong with every color he saw. The woman's silence enraged him, but the rage was like something happening to another person. The odd feeling of detachment persisted even after he recognized it.

"You act like a woman who needs violence," Joao

said. "Would you like to be turned over to my men? They're a little tired of you."

He found the words strange even as he spoke them—as though he'd wanted to say something else and these words had forced themselves out.

Rhin's face flamed. "You wouldn't dare!" she grated.

"Ah, we *can* speak," he said. "Don't be melodramatic, though. I wouldn't give you the pleasure."

Joao shook his head; that wasn't what he'd wanted to say at all.

Rhin glared at him. "You . . . insolent . . ."

Joao found himself producing a wolfish grin, saying, "Nothing you say will make me turn you over to my men."

The silence that followed was filled with sense of drawing apart—farther, farther. Joao felt that Rhin actually was growing smaller. He grew aware of a distant roaring, wondered if it was a sound in his own ears.

"That roaring," he said.

"Jefe?"

It was Vierho directly behind him.

"What is that roaring?" Joao asked.

"It's the river, Jefe; a chasm." Vierho pointed to a black rock escarpment rising distantly above the jungle. "When the wind is right we hear it. Jefe?"

"What is it?" Joao felt a surge of anger at Vierho. Why couldn't the man speak right out?

"A word with you, Jefe." Vierho drew him toward the blond Nordic who was standing outside one of the tents. The man's face looked gray except around the acid burn on his cheek.

Joao looked back at Rhin. She had turned away from him, stood with her arms folded. The stiffness of her back, the pose, all of it struck Joao as almost humorous. He suppressed laughter, allowed himself to be led up to the blond fellow. What had she called him? Ahh, Hogar. Yes, Hogar.

"The gentleman here"—Vierho indicated Hogar— "says the female doctor was bitten by insects that got past their barriers."

"The first night," Hogar whispered.

"She has not been the same since," Vierho said. "In the head, you understand? We humor her, Jefe, no?"

Joao wet his lips with his tongue. He felt dizzy and warm.

"The insects that bit her were similar to the ones that were on you," Hogar said. His voice sounded apologetic.

He's making fun of me! Joao thought.

"I wish to see Chen-Lhu," Joao said. "At once."

"He was very badly poisoned and burned," Hogar said. "We think he's dying."

"Where is he?"

"In the tent here, but I . . ."

"Is he conscious?"

"Senhor Martinho, he is conscious but not in condition for any prolonged . . ."

"I give the orders here!" Joao snapped.

An odd look passed between Hogar and Vierho.

Vierho said, "Jefe, perhaps . . ."

"I will see Doctor Chen-Lhu now!" Joao said. He brushed past Hogar and into the tent.

The place was a gloomy hole after the morning sunlight outside. It took an instant for Joao's eyes to adjust themselves. In that instant, Hogar and Vierho joined him in the tent.

"Please, Senhor Martinho," Hogar said.

Vierho said, "Jefe, perhaps later."

"Who is there?"

The voice was low, but controlled, and came from a

cot at the far end of the tent. Joao made out the form
of a human figure stretched on the cot, the white marks
of bandages, recognized Chen-Lhu's face in the half
light.

"It is Joao Martinho," Joao said.

"Ahh, Johnny," Chen-Lhu said, and his voice sounded
stronger.

Hogar passed Joao, knelt beside the cot, said, "Please,
Doctor, do not excite yourself."

The words held an odd ring of familiarity for Joao,
but he couldn't place the association. He crossed to the
cot, looked down at Chen-Lhu. The man's cheeks were
sunken as though after a long famine. His eyes appeared
immersed in two black pits.

"Johnny," Chen-Lhu said, his voice a whisper. "We
are rescued, then."

"We are *not* rescued," Joao said. And he wondered
why the fool prattled so.

"Ahhh, too bad," Chen-Lhu said. "Then we'll all go
together, eh?" Chen-Lhu asked. And he thought: *What
irony! My scapegoat caught in the same trap. What fu-
tility!*

"There's still hope," Hogar said.

Joao saw Vierho cross himself, thought: *Silly fool!*

"While there's life, eh?" Chen-Lhu asked. He stared
up at Joao. "I'm dying, Johnny, but most of my past
eludes me." And he thought: *We'll all die here. And in
my homeland—they'll all die there, too. Starvation or
poison, what's the difference?*

Hogar looked at Joao, said, "Senhor, please go."

"No," Chen-Lhu said. "Stay. I've things to tell you."

"You mustn't tire yourself, sir," Hogar said.

"What difference?" Chen-Lhu asked. "We've
marched to the West, eh, Johnny? I wish I could laugh!"

Joao shook his head. His back ached and tingling

sensations ran along the skin of both arms. The interior of the tent seemed suddenly brighter.

"Laugh?" Vierho whispered. "Mother of God!"

"You want to know why my government won't let in your observers?" Chen-Lhu asked. "Such a joke! The Great Crusade has backfired in my land. The earth goes barren. Nothing helps it—fertilizers, chemicals, nothing."

Joao experienced difficulty assembling the words into meaningful form. *Barren? Barren?*

"We face such a famine as history has never seen," Chen-Lhu rasped.

"Is it the lack of insects?" Vierho whispered.

"Of course!" Chen-Lhu said. "What else has changed? We've broken key links in the ecological chain. Of course. We even know what links . . . now that it's too late."

Barren earth, Joao thought. It was a very interesting idea, but his head felt too hot to explore the thought.

Vierho, dismayed by Joao's silence, bent over Chen-Lhu, said, "Why don't your people admit this thing and warn the rest of us before it's too late?"

"Don't be a fool!" Chen-Lhu said, and there was some of the old, harsh command in his voice. "We'd lose all before we'd lose that much face. I tell it here now because I'm dying and because none of you will survive me for long."

Hogar stood up and stepped back from the cot as though fearful of contamination.

"We need a scapegoat, you see?" Chen-Lhu said. "That's why I was sent here—to find us a scapegoat. We're fighting for more than our lives."

"You could always blame the Northamericans," Hogar said, his tone bitter.

"I fear we've worn that one out, even with our people," Chen-Lhu said. "We did the thing ourselves, you see? There's no escaping that. No . . . all we could hope for was to find here a way of blaming someone else. The British and French provided some of our poisons. We explored that with no success. Some Russian teams helped us . . . but the Russians haven't realigned their entire country—only to the Ural Line. They could show the same problems as we have and . . . you see? They'd make us appear foolish."

"Why haven't the Russians said anything?" Hogar asked.

Joao looked at Hogar, thinking: *Senseless words, senseless words.*

"The Russians are quietly rolling back their Ural line into the Green," Chen-Lhu said. "Re-infesting, you see? No . . . my last orders were to find a new insect, typically Brazilian, that would destroy many of our crops . . . and for whose presence we could blame . . . who? Perhaps some bandeirantes."

Blame bandeirantes, Joao thought. *Yes, everyone is blaming the bandeirantes.*

"The really amusing thing," Chen-Lhu said, "is what I see in your Green. Do you know what I see?"

"You're a devil!" Vierho grated.

"No, just a patriot," Chen-Lhu said. "Are you not curious as to what I see in your Green?"

"Speak and be damned!" Vierho said.

That's telling him, Joao thought.

"I see the signs in your Green of the same blight that has struck my poor nation," Chen-Lhu said. "Smaller fruit, smaller crops—smaller leaves, paler plants. It's slow at first, but everyone will see it soon."

"Then maybe they'll stop before it's too late," Vierho said.

That's foolishness, Joao thought. *Who ever stops before it's too late?*

"Such a simple fellow you are," Chen-Lhu said. "Your rulers are the same as mine: they see nothing but their own survival. They will see nothing else *until* it's too late. This is always the way with governments."

Joao wondered why the tent was growing so dark after being so bright. He felt hot and his head whirled as though he'd had too much alcohol. A hand touched his shoulder. He looked down at it, followed the hand up to an arm . . . a face: Rhin. There were tears in her eyes.

"Joao . . . Senhor Martinho, I've been such a fool," she said.

"You heard?" Chen-Lhu asked.

"I heard," she said.

"A pity," Chen-Lhu said. "I'd hoped to preserve some of your illusions . . . for a little while, anyway."

What an odd conversation, Joao thought. *What an odd person, this Rhin. What an odd place, this tent with its ridge-pole coming around to face me.*

Something thuded against his back and his head.

I've fallen, he thought. *Isn't that odd?*

The last thing he heard before unconsciousness flooded his mind with black ink was Vierho's startled voice:

"Jefe!"

There was a dream in which Rhin hovered over him saying, "What difference does it make who gives the orders?" And in the dream, he could only turn a baleful stare on her and think how hateful she looked—in spite of her beauty.

Someone said, "What's the difference? We'll all be dead soon anyway."

And another voice said, "Look, there's a new one. That one looks like Gabriel Martinho, the Prefect."

Joao felt himself sinking into a void where his face was held by clamps that forced him to stare into the monitor screen on the dash of his airtruck's pod. The screen showed a giant stag beetle with the face of his father. And the sound was a cicada hum up and down the scale with a voice inside the hum: "Don't excite yourself. Don't excite yourself . . ."

He awoke screaming to realize there was no sound in his throat—only the memory of screams. His body was bathed in perspiration. Rhin sat beside him wiping his forehead. She looked pale and thin, her eyes sunken. For a moment he wondered if this emaciated Rhin Kelly were part of a dream; she seemed to give no notice to the fact that his eyes were open although she looked right at him.

He tried to speak, but his throat was too dry.

The movement attracted Rhin, though. She bent over him, peered into his eyes. Presently she reached behind her, brought up a canteen, trickled a few drops of water down his throat.

"What . . ." he croaked.

"You had the same thing that hit me, but more of it," she said. "A nerve drug in the insect venom. Don't try to exert yourself."

"Where?" he asked.

She looked at him, sensing the broader question. "We're still in the same old trap," she said, "but now we have a chance of getting out."

His eyes spoke the question that his lips couldn't form.

"Your truck pod," she said. "Some of its circuits were badly damaged, but Vierho rigged substitutes. Now be quiet a moment."

She checked his pulse, put a blood-gauge thermometer against his neck, read it. "Fever's down," she said. "Have you ever had heart trouble of any kind?"

Instantly he thought of his father; but this question wasn't directed to his father.

"No," he whispered.

"I have a very few energy packs," she said. "Direct feed. I can give you one if you don't have a weak heart."

"Do it," he said.

"I'll use a vein in your leg," she said. "They gave it to me on the left arm and I saw blue and red lights for an hour." She bent to a case beside the cot, took a flat black cartridge from it, pulled the blanket off his feet and began applying the energy pack to his left leg.

He could feel her working there, but it was so far away and he was so drowsy.

"This is how we brought Dr. Chen-Lhu around," she said, pulling the blanket back over his feet.

Travis didn't die, he thought. He felt that this was an extremely important fact, but couldn't place the reason.

"It was more than the nerve drug, of course," she said. "With Dr. Chen-Lhu and with me, that is. Vierho spotted it in the water."

"Water?"

She took the word as a request, dribbled more water down his throat from the canteen.

"Our second night here we dug a well in one of the tents," she said. "River seepage, naturally. Water's loaded with poisons, some of them ours. That's what Vierho tasted: the bitterness. But my tests shows there's something else in that water: a hallucinogenic that produces a reaction very like schizophrenia. It isn't anything humans put there."

Joao could feel energy pumping into him from the

pack on his leg. A cramp like acute hunger knotted his stomach. When it passed, he said, "Something from . . . *them.*"

"Very likely," she said. "We've rigged a crude still. There's a variable resistance to this hallucinogenic. Hogar appears to be completely immune, but he didn't get any of the venom drug. *That* seems to leave you wide open."

Again she checked his pulse.

"Are you feeling stronger?"

"Yes."

The cramps were in the muscles of his thighs now—rhythmic and painful. They receded.

"We've analyzed that skeleton in your pod," she said. "An amazing thing. Remarkably like a human skeleton except for ridges and tiny holes—presumably where the insects attach themselves and articulate it. It's bird-light but very strong. The kinship to chitin is quite apparent."

Joao thought about this, letting the energy from the pack on his leg accumulate. He was feeling stronger by the second. So much seemed to have happened, though: the pod repaired, that skeleton analyzed.

"How long have I been here?" he asked.

"Four days," she said. She glanced at her wristwatch. "Almost to the hour. It's still fairly early."

Joao grew aware then of the forced cheerfulness in her tone. What was she hiding? Before he could explore the question, a hiss of fabric and brief flash of sunlight told of someone entering the tent.

Chen-Lhu appeared behind Rhin. The Chinese seemed to have aged fifty years since Joao had last seen him. Skin sagged and wrinkled at his jawline. The cheeks were concave pockets. He walked with a fragile caution.

"I see the patient is awake," he said.

The voice surprised Joao by its strength—as though all the man's physical energy had been channeled into this one aspect of him.

"He's under pack right now," she said.

"Wise," Chen-Lhu said. "There isn't much time. Have you told him?"

"Only that we've repaired his truck pod."

This must be phrased very delicately, Chen-Lhu thought. *Very delicately. Latin honor can shoot off at strange tangents.*

"We are going to attempt escaping in your pod," Chen-Lhu said.

"How can we?" Joao asked. "That pod won't lift more than three people at the most."

"Three people is all it'll carry, that is correct," Chen-Lhu said. "But it won't be required to lift them; in fact, it cannot lift them."

"What do you mean?"

"Your landing was rather rough: one of your float-skids is damaged and you ruptured the belly tank. Most of the fuel was gone before we discovered the damage. There's also the matter of controls: they're not of the best, even after the Padre's most ingenious ministrations."

"That still means only three people in it," Joao said.

"If we can't transmit a message, we can carry it," Rhin said.

Good girl, Chen-Lhu thought. He waited for Joao to absorb this.

"Who?" Joao asked.

"Myself," Chen-Lhu said. "Only for the reason that I can testify to the debacle in my nation, warn your people before it's too late."

Chen-Lhu's words brought an entire conversation flooding back into Joao's awareness—in the tent: Hogar, Vierho . . . Chen-Lhu babbling about . . . about . . .

"Barren earth," Joao said.

"Your people must learn before it's too late," Chen-
Lhu said. "So I will be one of the passengers. And Rhin
here because . . ." He managed a weak shrug. ". . . because of chivalry, I would say, but also because she's re-
sourceful."

"That's two," Joao said.

"And you will make three," Chen-Lhu said, and he
waited for the outburst.

But Joao merely said, "That doesn't make sense." He
lifted his head, stared down along the length of his body
on the cot. "Four days here and . . ."

"But you're the one with *pistolao*—political connec-
tions," Rhin said. "You can make people listen."

Joao dropped his head back onto the cot.

"My own father wouldn't even listen to me!"

The statement evoked a surprising silence. Rhin
looked up at Chen-Lhu, back to Joao.

"You have your own political pipelines, Travis," Joao
said. "Probably better than mine."

"And perhaps not," Chen-Lhu said. "Besides, you're
the one who saw this creature close up, the one whose
skeleton we will take back with us. You are the eye-
witness."

"We're all eye-witnesses."

"It was put to a vote," Rhin said. "Your men insist."

Joao looked from Rhin to Chen-Lhu, back to Rhin.
"That still leaves twelve men here. What happens to
them?"

"Only eight now," Rhin whispered.

"Who?" Joao managed.

"Hogar," she said. "Thome of your crew; two of my
field aides: Cardin and Lewis."

"How?"

"There is a thing that looks like a qena flute," Chen-Lhu said. "The creature in your truck pod carried one."

"Dart gun," Joao said.

"No," Chen-Lhu said. "They mimic us better than that. It's a generator of a sonic-disruption pattern. What it disrupts is human red blood cells. They must get fairly close with it, though, and we've been keeping them back since we discovered it."

"You can see we have to get this information out," Rhin said.

No doubt of that, Joao thought.

"Surely there must be someone stronger, better able to insure the success of this," Joao said.

"You'll be as strong as any of us in a couple of hours," Rhin said. "We are not in the best condition, none of us."

Joao stared up at the gray light of the tent ceiling. *Very little rocket fuel, damaged controls. They mean to make for the river, of course: float out in the pod. It'll afford some protection from those . . . things.*

Rhin stood up. "You rest and build up your strength," she said. "I'll bring you some food in a little while. We have nothing but field rations, but at least they're loaded with energy."

What river is that? Joao wondered. *The Itapura, very likely.* He made a rough estimate based on his knowledge of the region and the length of his flight over it before the crash landing here. *It'll be seven or eight hundred kilometers by river! And we're right on top of the rainy season. We don't stand a chance.*

6

The dancing pattern of insects on the cave ceiling appeared as a lovely thing to the Brain. It admired the interplay of color and motion while it read the patterned message:

"Report from listeners in the savannah; acknowledge."

The Brain signaled for the dance to proceed.

"Three humans prepare to flee in the small vehicle," danced the insects. "The vehicle will not fly. They will try to escape by floating away on the river. What do we do?"

The Brain paused to assess data. The trapped humans had been under observation twelve days. They'd provided much information about their reactions under stress. The information expanded data obtained from captives under more direct control. Ways to immobilize and kill humans became more obvious daily. But the problem wasn't how to kill them. It was how to communicate with them in the absence of fear or stress on either side.

Some of the humans—like the old one with the grand manner—made offers and suggestions and *appeared* to display reason . . . but could they be trusted? That was the key question.

The Brain felt a desperate need for observational data on humans under conditions it could control without that control being noticed. Discovery of the listening posts in the Green had aroused a frenzy of human activity. They used new sonotoxics, deepened their barriers, renewed their attacks on the Red.

Another worry compounded all this—the unknown fate of four units which had penetrated the barriers before the Bahia catastrophe. Only one had returned; its report: "We became twelve. Six gave up unit-identity to envelop the area where we captured the two human leaders. Their fate is unknown. One unit was destroyed. Four dispersed to produce more of us."

Discovery of those four units at this time would be catastrophe, the Brain realized.

When would the simulacra emerge? That depended on local conditions—temperature, available foods, chemicals, moisture. The lone unit that had returned had no knowledge of where the four had gone.

We must find them! the Brain thought.

The problems of individually-directed action dismayed the Brain then. The simulacra were a mistake. Many identical units would only attract disastrous attention.

That the simulacra meant no great harm and were conditioned only to limited violence had no meaning under present conditions. That they wanted only to be allowed to speak and to reason with human leaders—this plan carried only pathos and irony now.

The reported words of the human called Chen-Lhu came back to plague the Brain: "*Debacle . . . barren earth."* This Chen-Lhu offered a way to solve their mutual problem, but what were his true intentions? Could he be trusted?

The Brain suspended decision, directed a question at its minions: "Which humans will try to escape?"

Attention must be paid to such details, the Brain knew. Hive orientation tended to ignore individuals. The error with the simulacra had originated in this tendency.

On the surface, the Brain knew its problem appeared deceptively simple. But just under the surface lay the hellish complications of emotional triggers. *Emotions! Emotions!* Reason had so many barriers to hurdle.

The messengers had consulted their listening-post data. Now they danced out the name sounds: "The latent queen, Rhin Kelly, and the ones called Chen-Lhu and Joao Martinho."

Martinho, the Brain thought. That was the human from the other half of the airtruck. In this fact lay an indication of the humans' complicated quasi-hive kinship. There could be value in that relationship. And Chen-Lhu would be in the vehicle, as well.

The insects on the ceiling, having been bred with a repeat factor to insure communication, repeated their previous question:

"What counter action is required?"

"Message to all units," the Brain said. "The three in the vehicle will be allowed to escape to the river. Offer just enough resistance to make it appear we oppose the escape. They are to be followed by action groups capable of disposing of them whenever necessary. As soon as the three have reached the river, overwhelm the ones who remain."

Messenger units began assembling overhead, dancing the pattern to imprint it. They took off in compact groups, darting out of the cavemouth into the sunlight.

The Brain admired the color and motion for a few minutes, then lowered its sensors, set itself to the problem of overcoming protein incompatibility.

We must produce immediate and consequential benefits that the humans cannot fail to recognize, the Brain thought. *If we can demonstrate dramatic usefulness, they may yet be brought to understand that interdependence is circular, inextricably entangled and a matter of life and death.*

They need us and we need them . . . but the burden of proof has fallen on us. And if we fail to prove it, this will be truly barren earth.

"It will be dark soon, Jefe," Vierho said. "You will go then." Vierho swung the pod's canopy forward, leaned into it.

Joao stood one step behind him, still feeling weak and plagued by occasional flash-cramps in his left leg above the energy pack. The direct feed and specialized hormones could only approximate the needs of a specific body, and Joao could feel himself half poised against strange tensions because of this treatment.

"I have put the food and other emergency supplies here under the seat," Vierho said. "There's more food in the gig-box there in the back. You have two spray-rifles with twenty spare charges, one hard-pellet carbine. I'm sorry we have so little ammo for it. There're a dozen foamal bombs under the other seat, and I've tied a handspray rig into the corner back there. It's fully charged."

Vierho straightened, glanced back at the tents. His voice fell to a conspiratorial whisper. "Jefe, I do not trust the Doctor Chen-Lhu. I heard him when he thought he was dying. This new face is not like him."

"It's a chance we have to take," Joao said. "I still think you or one of the others who weren't as sick should go in place of me."

"No more talk of that, Jefe, please."

Again Vierho's voice fell to the conspiratorial whisper: "Jefe, step close to me as though we are saying goodbye."

Joao hesitated, then obeyed. He felt something metallic and heavy pushed into the belt pocket of his uniform. The pocket sagged with it. Joao pulled his jungle jacket around to cover the sag, whispered, "What's that?"

"It belonged to my great grandfather," Vierho said. "It is a pistol called the .475 Magnum. It has five bullets and here are two dozen more." Another packet was slipped into the side pocket of Joao's jacket. "It's not much good except against men," Vierho said.

Joao swallowed, felt tears dampen his eyes. All the Irmandades knew the Padre carried that old blunderbuss and wouldn't part with it. The fact that he parted with it now meant he expected to die here—likely true.

"God go with you, Jefe," Vierho said.

Joao turned, looked to the river about five hundred meters away across the savannah. He could just glimpse the beach of the opposite shore, the wild growth there illuminated by the afternoon sun. The jungle lifted there in steady waves of color, its bold lines standing out in the flat light. The growth was a deep blue-green at the bottom, a sun-bleached sage at the top, and with flecks of yellow, red and ochre between. Above the green towered a candello tree with batfalcon nests cluttering the forks of its branches. A twisted screen of lianas partly obscured a wall of mata-polo trees to the left.

"Fifteen minutes of fuel in the pod and that's all?" Joao asked.

"Maybe a minute more, Jefe."

We'll never make it with nothing but that river's current to move us, Joao thought.

"Jefe, sometimes there's a wind on the river," Vierho said.

Christ, he doesn't expect us to sail that thing, does he? Joao wondered. He looked at Vierho, saw the deep weariness in the man's face, the scarecrow emaciation.

"That wind could cause trouble, Jefe," Vierho said. "I have used one of the pod's grapnel anchors to make a thing that will float just under the surface and provide some drag. It is called a sea anchor. It'll keep the nose of the pod into the wind."

"That's a clever idea, Padre," Joao said.

And he wondered: *Why do we play out this farce? We're going to die here, all of us ... either here or somewhere down that river.* There were seven or eight hundred kilometers of that river—rapids, chasms, waterfalls—and the rainy season was almost on them. The river would become a torrential hell. And if it didn't get them, there were always the new insects, the creatures of acid and sophisticated poisons.

"You better inspect it one more time yourself, Jefe," Vierho said. He gestured at the pod.

Yes, anything to keep busy, to keep from thinking, Joao thought. He'd already been over it once, but another look wouldn't hurt anything. After all, their lives would depend on it ... for awhile.

Our lives!

Joao allowed himself to wonder then if escape were possible, if there were any hope at all. This was, after all, the pod of a jungle airtruck. It could be sealed against most insects. It was designed to take abuse.

I mustn't allow myself to hope, he thought.

But he set himself to another inspection of the pod . . . just in case.

The white bandeirante paint of its exterior had been washed away in patches, streaked and etched by acid. The float skids, normally long and faired extrusions of the pod's bottom curve, had been cranked out manually and locked in position. They formed a flat step up to the stub wings and into the cabin. The entire pod was just short of five and a half meters long with two meters at the rear taken up by the rocket motors. The motor complex which had nested into the discarded rear truck section was cut off flat on both sides. The pod itself was roughly oval in cross section. This left two flat half-moon surfaces which opened into the rear bulkhead of the pod's cabin. The left-side half-moon was a maze of male and female connectors which once had linked the pod to the truck section. The right side was sealed by a hatch which now opened from the cabin and down to one of the float skids.

Joao inspected the hatch, made certain the connectors had all been sealed off, looked at the right-side float skid. A jagged rent in the side of the float had been patched with butyl and fabric.

He could smell rocket fuel, and he knelt to peer up at the belly tank section. Vierho had siphoned out the fuel, applied a chemical hotpatch on the outside and spraytank sealant inside, then replaced the fuel.

"It should hold all right if you don't hit anything," Vierho said.

Joao nodded, worked his way around, climbed up on the left stub wing and looked down into the cabin. Dual control seats forward and the padded gig-box in the rear. Spray stains were all over the interior. The interior formed a space about two meters square and two and a half meters deep. Windows in front looked down over the rounded nose. Side windows stopped at the wings forward, dipped deeper in the rear. A single transparent panel of polarizing plastic ran over the top to the rear bulkhead.

Joao let himself down into the command seat on the left, checked the manual controls. They felt loose and sluggish. New fuel-monitoring and firing controls had been installed with crude, hand-lettered labels.

Vierho spoke at his shoulder.

"I had to use whatever was available, Jefe. There was not much. I'm glad these IEO people were such fools."

"Hmmm?" Joao spoke absently as he continued his examination.

"When they left their truck, they took tents. I would've taken more weapons. But the tents gave me the new guy cables and fabric for patches."

Joao finished tracing the fuel controls. "No automatic demand valves on the fuel lines," he said.

"They couldn't be repaired, Jefe—but you don't have much fuel anyway."

"Enough to blow us all to hell . . . or run away with us if it gets out of hand."

"That's why I put the big knob there, Jefe; I told you about that. On and off in short bursts—no problem."

"Unless I accidentally give it too big a drink."

"Underneath there, Jefe: the piece of wood, that's the stop I put in. I tested it with containers under the fuel injectors. You won't have a very fast ship . . . but it's enough."

"Fifteen minutes," Joao mused.

"That's just a guess, Jefe."

"I know—maybe a hundred and fifty kilometers if everything works as it's supposed to; a hundred and fifty meters with us spread all over if it doesn't."

"A hundred and fifty kilometers," Vierho said. "You

wouldn't even be halfway to civilization."

"No argument," Joao said. "I was just thinking out loud."

"Well, is everything ready to go?" Chen-Lhu's voice boomed up at them full of false heartiness. Joao looked down to see the man standing near the tip of the left wing, his body bent over with the appearance of weakness. Joao had just about decided Chen-Lhu's weakness was appearance only.

He was the first to recover, Joao thought. *He's had more time to regain his strength. But . . . he was closer to death. Maybe I'm just imagining things.*

"Is it ready or isn't it?" Chen-Lhu asked.

"I hope so," Joao said.

"There's danger?"

"It'll be like a Sunday ride in the park," Joao said.

"Is it time to come aboard?"

Joao looked at the shadows stretching out from the tents, the orange cast of the sunlight. He found he was having difficulty breathing, knew this for tension. Joao took a deep breath, found a level of hesitant calm within himself; not relaxed, certainly, but with fear held at bay.

Vierho answered for Joao: "Twenty minutes, more or less, Senhor Doctor." He patted Joao's shoulder. "Jefe, my prayers go with you."

"You sure you wouldn't rather take my place, Padre?"

"We will not discuss it, Jefe." Vierho stepped down off the float skid.

Rhin Kelly emerged from her lab tent with a small bag in her left hand, crossed to stand beside Chen-Lhu.

"About twenty minutes, my dear," Chen-Lhu said.

"I'm not at all sure I should have a place in that thing," she said. "One of the others might give you a . . ."

"It has been decided," Chen-Lhu said, and he put angry sharpness in his voice. *The fool woman! Why can't she let well enough alone?* "No one will permit you to stay," he said. *Besides, my dear Rhin, I may need you to sway that Brazilian. This Joao Martinho will have to be played very carefully. A woman sometimes can do that better than a man.*

"I'm still not sure," she said.

Chen-Lhu looked up at Joao. "Perhaps you should speak to her, Johnny. Surely you don't want to leave her here."

Here or there—not much difference, Joao thought. But he said, "As you say: the decision already has been made. You'd better get aboard and fasten your safety harness."

"Where do you want us?" Chen-Lhu asked.

"You in back; you're heavier," Joao said. "I don't think we'll get off the ground before we hit the river, but we might. I want us nose high."

"Do you want us both in back?" Rhin asked. And she realized then that she had agreed with their decision. *Why not?* she asked herself, not realizing she shared Joao's pessimism.

"Jefe?"

Joao looked down at Vierho, who'd just completed a final examination of the undercarriage.

Rhin and Chen-Lhu went around to the right side, began climbing in.

"How does it look?" Joao asked.

"Try to hold it up on that left skid a little, Jefe," Vierho said. "That might help."

"Right."

Rhin began strapping herself into the bucket seat beside him.

"We'll send help as soon as we can," Joao said, sensing how empty and useless the words were as soon as he spoke them.

"Of course, Jefe."

Vierho stepped back, readied a bomb thrower.

Thome and the others came out of the tents, loaded with weapons, began setting them up on the side facing the river.

No good-byes, Joao thought. *Yes, that's best. Treat this as routine, just another flight.*

"Rhin, what's in that little overnight bag you brought?" Chen-Lhu asked.

"Personal things . . . and . . ." She swallowed. "Some of the men gave me some letters to take."

"Ahhh," Chen-Lhu said, "an appropriate and touching bit of sentimentality."

"What's wrong with it?" Joao growled.

"Nothing," Chen-Lhu said. "That's just it: nothing is wrong with it."

Vierho returned to the wingtip, said, "Just as we planned, Jefe—when you give the signal that you're ready, we'll lay down a foamal barrage along your path. That should stall them long enough for you to make it onto the river, and it'll make the grass out there more slippery."

Joao nodded, began rehearsing the flight routine in his mind. None of the switches were exactly where they should be. Igniter to the left now; throttle knob jutting from the dash instead of on the floor between the seats. He set the trim tabs, adjusted the feather-slots in the ailerons.

A pre-dark hush had fallen over the savannah. The grass stretched out ahead of them like a green sea. The river out there was only about fifty meters across: a narrow path for him to hit if the pod got up too much speed. There'd be no dusk at this latitude and altitude,

Joao knew. He'd have to gauge his moment carefully, using the last of the light for the dash across the savannah—and darkness to shield them once they hit the river.

A fifteen-meter range for those acid-shooting insects, Joao thought. *That only leaves us a narrow strip down the middle if they attack from shore. And God alone knows what other forms they may be able to hit us with—flying creatures, water skaters . . .*

"Stand by with sprayrifles as soon as we're safely on the river," he said. "They may mount an all-out attack once they see us trying to escape."

"We'll be ready," Chen-Lhu said. "The rifles are in this gig-box under me, not so?"

"Right."

Joao lowered the canopy, sealed it. "This model has self-sealing rifle ports on both sides where the windows dip just behind the wings," he said. "See them?"

"Clever design," Chen-Lhu said.

"Vierho's idea," Joao said. "It's in all our pods." He waved to Vierho, who returned to the bomb thrower.

Joao turned on the pod's landing lights.

All the men saw the signal; a shower of rifle spray arched out toward the river. Foamal bombs began landing along the track they'd take.

Joao punched the igniter, saw the safety light go on. He waited, counting three seconds before the light dimmed and went out. *Not too bad*, he thought, and he eased the throttle knob ahead.

The rocket motors came on with a jarring blast that had them over the perimeter ditch and roaring toward the river before Joao could ease off the feed. With a sense of breathless shock, he realized they were airborne. The pod felt sluggish, though, and with a tendency to fishtail—too much drag from the floats. They weren't meant to be left out there in flight.

There was no time for flying niceties, though. Joao wrenched the nose around, aimed for a stretch of river where the savannah blended into jungle on both sides. The river was a long pool there, wider, pointing toward blue hills in the background. There came a moment of gliding suspense. Floats touched the river in a cushioned bounce . . . up, down . . . spray on both sides . . . slower, slower.

The nose came down.

It was only then that Joao remembered he had to favor the right side float.

The pod was still making forward speed, but coasting slower and slower.

Joao held his breath, wondering if the patch had been torn off, waiting for the right side to start its tipping plunge into the river.

The pod remained level.

"Have we made it?" Rhin asked. "Are we really out of there?"

"I think so," Joao said, and he cursed the surge of hope that had accompanied that brief flight.

Chen-Lhu passed sprayrifles forward, said, "We seem to've caught them by surprise. Ah, ah! Look back!"

Joao whirled as far as his safety harness would permit, looked back across the savannah. Where the distant cluster of tents had been there now rolled a gray mound that heaved and extruded odd protuberances which flailed and subsided.

With a deep shudder, Joao realized the mound was composed of billions of insects overwhelming the camp.

An eddy caught the pod, turned it away from the scene as though some instinct within Joao controlled the motion to remove from view a thing he no longer could bear to see. For a moment the river shimmered ahead of him with a glassy orange haze. Then night blotted the view. The sky became a luminous silver with a thin slice of moon.

Vierho, Joao thought. *Thome . . . Ramon . . .*

Tears blurred his eyes.

"Oh, God!" Rhin said.

"God, hah!" Chen-Lhu barked. "Another name for the movement of fate!"

Rhin buried her face in her hands. She felt that she was up for try-out in some cosmic drama, without script or rehearsal, without words or music, without knowing her role.

God is a Brazilian, Joao thought, calling to mind his nation's old expression of self confidence touched by fear. *At night, God corrects the errors Brazilians make during the day.*

What was it Vierho had always said. *"Believe in the Virgin and run."*

Joao felt a sprayrifle across his lap, the metal cold against his hands.

I couldn't have helped them, he thought. *The range was too great.*

7

"You said the vehicle would not fly!" the Brain accused.

Its sensors probed the messenger pattern on the cave ceiling, listened for the afferent hum that might expand the meaning. But the configuration revealed on the ceiling by the phosphor-light of servant insects remained firm, as steady as the patch of stars standing in the cavemouth beyond the messengers.

Chemical demands pulsed through the Brain, sending its servant nurses into a frenzy of ministrations. This was the closest to consternation the Brain had ever experienced. Its logical awareness labeled the experience as an emotion and sought parallel references even while it worked on the substance of the report.

The vehicle flew only a short distance and landed on the river. It remains on the river with its thrusting force dormant.

But it can fly!

The first serious doubt of its information entered the Brain's computations then. The experience was a form of alienation from the creations which had created it.

"The claim that the vehicle would not fly came directly from the humans," the messengers danced. "Their assessment was reported."

It was a pragmatic statement, more to fill out the report predicting the escape try than to defend against the Brain's accusation.

That fact should have been part of the original report, the Brain thought. *The messengers must be taught not to intervene, but report all details complete with weight-by-source. But how can this be done? They're creatures of firm reflex and tied to a self-limiting system.*

Obviously new messengers would have to be designed and bred.

With this thought, the Brain moved even further from its creators. It understood then how an *action-of-mimicry,* a pure reflex, gave birth to itself, but the Brain, the *thing-produced-by-reflex,* was having an inevitable feedback effect, changing the original reflexes which had created it.

"What must be done about the vehicle on the river?" the messengers asked.

With its new insight, the Brain saw how this question had been produced—out of survival reflex.

Survival must be served, it thought.

"The vehicle will be allowed to proceed temporarily," the Brain ordered. "There must be no visible sign of molestation for the time being, but we must prepare safeguards. A cluster of the new *little-deadlies* will be conveyed to the vehicle under the cover of night. They must be instructed to infiltrate every available hole on the vehicle and remain in hiding. They must not take action against the occupants of the vehicle without orders! But they must stand ready to destroy the occupants whenever necessary."

The Brain fell silent then, secure in the knowledge that its orders would be carried out. And it took up its new understanding to examine as though this were an autonomous fragment. The experience was both fascinating and terrifying because here, living within its single-self, was an element capable of debate and separate action.

Decisions—conscious decisions, the Brain thought, *these are a punishment inflicted upon the single-self by consciousness. There are conscious decisions that can fragment the singleself. How can humans stand up under such a load of decisions?*

Chen-Lhu tipped his head back, resting in the corner between the window and rear bulkhead, stared up at the melon-curve of moon lifting across the sky. The moon was the color of molten copper.

An acid-etched frost line ran diagonally down the window to the faired curve of exterior skin. Chen-Lhu's eyes followed the line and, for a moment as he stared at the place where the window ended beside him, he thought he saw a row of tiny dots, like barely visible gnats marching across the window.

In an eyeblink, they vanished.

Did I imagine them? he wondered.

He thought of alerting the others, but Rhin had been near hysteria for almost an hour now since witnessing the death of their camp. She'd have to be nursed back to usefulness.

I could've imagined them, Chen-Lhu thought. *Only the moon for illumination—spots in front of my eyes; nothing unusual about that.*

The river had narrowed here to no more than six or seven times the pod's wingspan. A shadowy wall of overhanging trees hemmed in the track of water.

"Johnny, turn on the wing lights for a few minutes," Chen-Lhu said.

"Why?"

"They'll see us if we do," Rhin said.

She heard the almost-hysteria in her own voice and was shocked by it. *I'm an entomologist,* she told herself. *Whatever's out there, it's just a variation on something familiar.*

But this reasoning lacked comfort. She realized that some primal fear had touched her, arousing instincts with which reason could not contend.

"Make no mistake," Chen-Lhu said, and he tried to speak softly, reasonably. "Whatever overwhelmed our friends . . . it knows where we are. I merely wish the light to confirm a suspicion."

"Are we being followed, eh?" Joao asked.

He snapped on the wing lights. The sudden glare picked out two caverns of brilliance that filled with fluttering, darting insects—a white-winged mob.

The current swung the pod around a bend. Their lights touched the river bank, outlined twisting medusa roots that clutched dark red clay, then swung with the vagaries of an eddy to pick out a narrow island—tall reeds and grass bending to the current, and the cold green reflections of eyes just above the water.

Joao snapped off the lights.

In the abrupt darkness, they heard the whining hum of insects and the metallic chime calls of river frogs . . . then, like a delayed comment, the coughing barks of a troop of red monkeys somewhere on the right shore.

The presence of the frogs and monkeys, Joao felt, carried a significance that he should understand. The significance eluded him.

Ahead, he could see bats flicker across the moonlit river, skimming the water to drink.

"They're following us . . . watching, waiting," Rhin said.

Bats, monkeys, frogs, all living intimately with the river, Joao thought. *But Rhin said the river carried poisons. Was there reason to lie about that?*

He tried to study her face in the dim reflections of moonlight that penetrated the cabin, but received only the impression of gaunt, withdrawn shadows.

"I think we are safe," Chen-Lhu said, "as long as we keep the cabin sealed and get our air through the vent filters."

"Open only in daylight," Joao said. "We can see what's around us then and use our rifles if we need to."

Rhin pressed her lips together to prevent them from trembling. She tipped her head back, looked up through the transparent strip across the roof of the cabin. A wilderness of stars flooded the sky, and when she lowered her gaze she could still see the stars—a shimmer of points, tremulous on the river surface. Quite suddenly the night filled her with a sensation of immense loneliness that was at the same time oppressive, holding her locked between the river's jungle walls.

The night was odorous with jungle smells that the vent filters could not remove. Every breath was thick with baited and repelling perfumes.

The jungle took on a form of conscious malignancy in her imagination. She sensed something out there in the night—a thinking entity which could swallow her without a moment's hesitation. The sense of reality with which her mind invested this image flowed over her and through her. She could give it no shape except immensity . . . but it was there.

"Johnny, how fast is the current along here?" Chen-Lhu asked.

Good question, Joao thought.

He bent forward to peer at the luminous dial of the altimeter. "Elevation here's eight hundred and thirty meters," he said. "If I've located us correctly on the right river, the channel drops about seventy meters in the next thirty kilometers." He worked the equation in his head. "I can only approximate, of course, but it'll be a six to eight knot current."

"Won't there be a search for us?" Rhin asked. "I keep thinking . . ."

"Don't think that way," Chen-Lhu said. "Any search, if it comes at all, will be for me—and not for several weeks. I knew where to look for you, Rhin." He hesitated, wondering if he was saying too much, giving Joao too many clues. "Only a few of my aides knew where I was going, and why."

Chen-Lhu hoped she'd hear the secrecy in his voice, get off this subject.

"You know how I got in here," Joao said. "If anybody thought to look for me . . . where'd they look?"

"But there's a chance, isn't there?" Rhin asked. Her voice revealed how desperately she wanted to believe in that chance.

"There is always a chance," Chen-Lhu said. And he thought: *You must calm yourself, Rhin. When I need you, there must be no problems of fear and hysteria.*

He set his mind then to the way Joao Martinho must be discredited if they reached civilization. Rhin's help would have to be enlisted in this enterprise, of course. Joao was the perfect scapegoat and this situation was made to order—if Rhin could be persuaded to help. Naturally, if she proved obstinate, she could be eliminated.

Midnight came to the cave above the river chasm before the Brain received its next report on the three humans and their floating vehicle.

Most of the conversation reported by the dancing messengers revealed only the tensions and pressures of the humans' circumstances. The humans realized, at least unconsciously, that they were in a loose trap. Most of this conversation could be set aside for later evaluation, but there was one matter for the Brain's immediate attention. The Brain felt something approaching chagrin that it had not anticipated this problem with its own logic.

"Enough action groups must be dispatched at once," the Brain ordered, "to accompany the vehicle but stay out of sight in the adjoining growth. These action groups must be ready to fly over the river whenever needed and hide the vehicle from any searchers or chance passersby in the sky above them."

One of the pod's stub wings brushed vines along the shore, awakening Joao from a light doze. He glanced back through the gloom to see Chen-Lhu alert and staring.

"It is time for you to awake and take your watch," Chen-Lhu said. "Rhin still sleeps."

"Have we been touching the shore very much like that?" Joao whispered.

"Not much."

"I should put out that sea anchor . . . Vierho made."

"That would not prevent us touching the shores. And it might snag on something and delay us."

"Padre covered the hooks on the grapnel. I don't think it'll snag. Wind's upriver right now, will be until morning. A drag in the water like that could speed us up."

"But how will you put it out there?"

"Yeah. . . ." Joao nodded. "Better wait until morning."

"It would be best, Johnny."

Rhin stirred restlessly.

Joao snapped on the winglights. Twin shafts of illumination leaped out to the jungle wall, revealed a cluster of sago palms in front of a screen of caña brava. The lights began to siphon in two flows of fluttering, darting insects.

"Our friends are still with us," Chen-Lhu whispered.

Joao turned off the lights.

Rhin began breathing in ragged gasps as though she were choking. Joao gripped her arm, spoke softly: "Are you all right?"

Without coming fully awake, Rhin felt his presence beside her, experienced a primitive demand for his protective masculinity. She nestled against him, murmured, "It's so hot. Doesn't it ever cool off?"

"She dreams," Chen-Lhu whispered.

"But it is hot," Joao said. He felt embarrassed by Rhin's obvious need for him, sensing that this amused and pleased Chen-Lhu.

"Towards morning we should get a little relief from the heat," Joao said. "Why don't you sleep for awhile, Travis?"

"Yes, I'll sleep now," Chen-Lhu said. He stretched out on the narrow gig-box, wondering: *Will I have to kill them? They are such fools, Rhin and Johnny . . . so obviously attracted to each other, but fighting it.*

The night breeze rocked the pod. Rhin nestled closer to Joao, breathing deeply, peacefully.

Joao stared out the windows.

The moon had gone down behind the hills, leaving only starlight to block out dark shadows along both shores. The hypnotic flow of dim shapes filled Joao with drowsiness. He concentrated on staying awake, peered through the black, his senses strained to the limit.

There was only the movement of the river and a hesitant rocking motion from the breeze.

The night awakened in Joao a sense of mystery. This river was haunted, peopled by the ghosts of every passenger it had ever carried, and now . . . by another presence. He could feel this other presence. The night was hushed with it. Even the frogs were silent.

Something barked in the jungle to the left. And Joao suddenly thought he heard a nerve beat of log drums. Distant . . . very distant: a still-vibration more felt than heard. It was gone before he could be sure.

The Indians were all cleared out of the Red, he thought. *Who could be using drums? I must've imagined it; my own pulse, that's what I heard.*

He held himself still, listening, but there was only Chen-Lhu's breathing, deep and even, and a small sigh from Rhin.

The river widened and its current slowed.

An hour passed . . . another. Time seemed dragged out by the current. A weary loneliness filled Joao. The pod around them felt fragile, inadequate: a corrupt and impermanent thing. He wondered how he had trusted his life to this machine high above the jungle when it was so vulnerable.

We'll never make it! he thought.

Chen-Lhu's voice, a low rumble, broke the silence: "This river, it is the Itacoasa, for sure, Johnny?"

"I'm reasonably certain of that," Joao whispered.

"What is the nearest civilization?"

"The bandeirante staging area at Santa Maria de Grao Cuyaba."

"Seven or eight hundred kilometers, eh?"

"More or less."

Rhin stirred in Joao's arms, and he felt himself responding to her femininity. He forced his mind to veer away from such thoughts, concentrated instead on the river ahead of them: a winding, twisting course with rapids and sunken limbs. It was a track menaced for its full length by that deadly presence which he sensed all around them. And there was one more peril he had not mentioned to the others: these waters abounded with cannibal fish, piranha.

"How many rapids ahead of us?" Chen-Lhu asked.

"I'm not sure," Joao said. "Eight or nine—maybe more. It depends on the season and height of water."

"We will have to use the fuel, fly across the rapids."

"This thing won't stand many takeoffs and landings," Joao said. "That right hand float . . ."

"Vierho did a good job; it'll suffice."

"We hope."

"You have sad thoughts, Johnny. That is no way to face this venture. How long to this Santa Maria?"

"Six weeks, with luck. Are you thirsty?"

"Yes. How much water do we have?"

"Ten liters . . . and we have the little pot still if we need more."

Joao accepted a canteen from Chen-Lhu, drank deeply. The water was warm and flat. He returned the canteen.

Far off, a night bird called, "Tuta! Tuta!" with a fluting voice.

"What was that?" Chen-Lhu hissed.

"A bird . . . nothing but a bird."

Joao sighed. The bird cry had filled him with foreboding, like an evil omen out of his superstitious past. A flux of night sounds pulsed in his temples. He stared out into darkness, saw a sudden witch light of fireflies along the right shore, smelled the wind from the jungle like an exhalation of evil breath.

The near hopelessness of their position pressed in

upon him. They stood at the edge of the rainy season, separated from any sanctuary by hundreds of kilometers of whirlpools and chasms. And they were the target of a cruel intelligence which used the jungle as a weapon.

A musk perfume lifted into his nostrils from Rhin. It left him with a profound awareness that she was female . . . and desirable.

The river tugged at the pod.

Joao felt then their alliance with the current dragging itself down to the sea like a black chord.

Another hour passed . . . and another.

Joao grew conscious of a red fireglow off to the right—dawn. The hoots and cries of howler monkeys greeted the light. Their uproar aroused birds to morning talk in the sheltered blackness of the forest: stacatto peepings, chirrings up and down the scale, intermittent screeches.

Pearl luster crept across the sky, became milk-silver light that gave definition to the world around the drifting pod. Joao looked out to the west, seeing foothills—one after another, piled waves of hills pounding against the Andean escarpment. He realized then that they had come down out of the first steep descent of the river to the high plateau.

The pod floated quietly like a great water bug against a backdrop of trees laced with the dancing flames of forest flowers. A sluggish current twisted into whorls against the floats. Curls of mist hung on the water like puffs of gauze.

Rhin awoke, straightened out of Joao's arms, stared downstream. The river was like a cathedral aisle between the tall trees.

Joao massaged his arm where Rhin's head had slowed the circulation. All the while, he studied the woman beside him. There was a small-child look about her: the red hair disarrayed, an unlined expression of innocence on her face.

She yawned, smiled at him . . . and abruptly frowned, coming fully awake to their situation. She shook her head, turned to look at Chen-Lhu.

The Chinese slept with his head thrown back into the corner. She had the sudden feeling that Chen-Lhu embodied fallen greatness, as though he were an idol out of his country's past. He breathed with a low, burred rasp. Heavy pores indented his skin and there was a burnt leather harshness to his complexion that she had never before noticed. A graying wheat stubble of hair stood out along his upper lip. She realized suddenly that Chen-Lhu dyed his hair. It was a touch of vanity that she had not suspected.

"There's not a breath of wind," Joao said.

"But it's cooler," she said.

She looked out the window on her side, saw wisps of reedy grass trailing from the float. The pod was twisting at the the push of every random current. The movement carried a certain majesty: slow sweeping turns like a formal dance to the river's rhythm.

"What do I smell?" she asked.

Joao sniffed: rocket fuel . . . very faint, the musk of human sweat . . . mildew. He knew without exploring it that mildew was the odor that had aroused her question.

"It's mildew," he said.

"Mildew?"

She looked around her at the interior of the cabin, seeing the smooth tan fabric of the ceiling edges, chrome on the instrument panel. She put her hands on the dual wheel of her side, moved it.

Mildew, she thought.

The jungle already had a beachhead inside here.

"We're almost into the rainy season, aren't we?" she said. "What'll that mean?"

"Trouble," he said. "High water . . . rapids."

Chen-Lhu's voice intruded: "Why look at the worst side?"

"Because we have to," she said.

Hunger awoke suddenly in Joao. His hands trembled; his mouth burned with thirst.

"Let's have a canteen," he said.

Chen-Lhu passed a canteen forward. It sloshed as Joao took it. He offered it to Rhin, but she shook her head, overcome by a strange sensation of nausea.

Poison in water conditioned me to a temporary rejection pattern, she thought. The sound of Joao drinking made her feel ill. How greedily he drank! She turned away, unable to look at him.

Joao returned the canteen to Chen-Lhu, thinking how secretively the man awoke. The first you knew about it was his voice, alert and intrusive. Chen-Lhu probably lay there pretending sleep, but awake and listening.

"I . . . I think I'm hungry," Rhin said.

Chen-Lhu produced ration packets and they ate in silence.

Now she felt thirst . . . and was surprised to have Chen-Lhu produce the canteen before she asked. He handed it to her. She knew then that he studied her and was aware of her emotions, saw many of her thoughts. It was a disquieting discovery. She drank in anger, thrust the canteen back at Chen-Lhu.

He smiled.

"Unless they're on the roof where we can't see them, or under the wings, our friends have left us," Joao said.

"So I've noticed," Chen-Lhu said.

Joao allowed his gaze to traverse both shores as far as he could see.

Not a movement of life.

Not a sound.

The sun had mounted high enough now to burn the mist off the river.

"It's going to be a hellish hot day in here," Rhin said.

Joao nodded.

The warmth had a definite moment of beginning, he thought. One instant it wasn't there, then it forced itself upon the senses. He released his safety harness, tipped his seat aside and slid into the rear of the cabin, put his hands on the dogs that sealed the rear hatch.

"Where're you going?" Rhin demanded. She blushed as she heard her own question.

Chen-Lhu chuckled.

She felt herself hating Chen-Lhu's callousness then, even when he tried to soften the effect of his reaction by saying, "We must learn certain blind spots of western conventionality, Rhin."

The derision was still there in his voice, and she heard it, whirled away.

Joao cracked open the hatch, examined the edges of it, inside and out. No obvious sign of insects. He looked down at the flat surface of the float extending to the rear beside the rocket motors—two and a half meters of low platform almost a meter wide. No sign of insects there.

He dropped down, closed the hatch.

As soon as the hatch closed, Rhin turned on Chen-Lhu.

"You are insufferable!" she blazed.

"Now, *Doctor* Kelly."

"Don't pull that we-professionals-together bit," she said. "You're still insufferable."

Chen-Lhu lowered his voice, said, "Before he comes back, we've a few things to discuss. There's no time for personalities. This is IEO business."

"The only IEO business we have is to carry your story to headquarters," she said.

He stared at her. This reaction had been predictable, of course, but a way had to be found to move her. *The Brazilians have a saying*, he thought, and said, "When you talk of duty, speak also of money."

"A conta foi paga por mim," she said. *"I paid that account."*

"I wasn't suggesting that *you* pay anything," he said.

"Are you offering to buy me?" she snapped.

"Others have," he said.

She glared at him. Was he threatening to tell Joao about her past in the IEO's investigative/espionage branch? Let him! But she'd learned a few things in the line of duty, and she assumed a look of uncertainty now. What did Chen-Lhu have in mind?

Chen-Lhu smiled. Westerners were always so susceptible to cupidity. "You wish to hear more?" he asked.

Her silence was acquiescence.

"For now," Chen-Lhu said, "you will ply your wiles upon Johnny Martinho, make him a slave of love. He must be reduced to a creature who'll do anything for you. For you, that should be fairly easy."

I've done it before, eh? she thought.

She turned away. *Well . . . I have done it before: in the name of duty.*

Chen-Lhu nodded to himself behind her. The patterns of life were unshakable. She'd come around—almost out of habit. The hatch beside him opened and Joao climbed up into the cabin.

"Not a sign of anything," he said, slipping back into his seat. "I left the hatch on half-lock in case anyone else wants to go out now."

"Rhin?" Chen-Lhu said.

She shook her head, took a shivering breath. "No."

"Then I'll avail myself of this opportunity," Chen-Lhu said. He opened the hatch, climbed down to the float closed the hatch.

Without turning, Rhin knew the hatch only appeared to be closed, that Chen-Lhu had left open a crack and had his ear to the opening. She stared straight ahead at the river's quicksilver track. The pod lay suspended in a blue vault of motionless air that slowly inflated with heat until she knew it must explode.

Joao looked at her. "You all right?"

There's a laugh! she thought.

A minute passed in silence.

"Something's wrong," Joao said. "You and Travis were whispering while I was out there. I couldn't make out what you said, but there was anger in your tone."

She tried to swallow in a dry throat. Chen-Lhu was listening to this, sure as hell. "I . . . he was teasing me."

"Teasing you?"

"Yes."

"About what?"

She turned away, studied the feathered softness of hills lifting to the right, and glimpsed far away there the snow cone of a mountain with a black tonsure of volcanic ash. Some of the mountain's serenity invaded her senses.

"About you," she said.

Joao looked at his hands, wondering why her admission embarrassed him.

In this silence, Rhin began to hum. She had a good voice and knew it: throaty, intimate. The voice was one of her best tools.

But Joao recognized the song and wondered at her choice. Even after she fell silent, the melody hung around him like a vapor. It was a native lament, a Lorca tragedy arranged for guitar:

> "Stay your whip, Old Death—
> It is not I who seeks your dark sea.
> I would not whine, nor beg—
> But ask it as one who has done your work.
> This river which is my life,
> Let it flow yet awhile in tranquility;
> For my love has gray smoke in her eyes . . .
> And farewells are difficult."

She'd only hummed the song, but the words were there, all the same.

Joao looked out to the left.

The river was lined here with mango trees, dense green foliage broken by the lighter sage of tropical mistletoe and occasional fur-coated *chonta* palms. Above the jungle's near reaches hovered two black and white *urubu* vultures. They hung in the burned-out steel blue sky as though painted there on a false backdrop.

The apparent tranquility of the scene held no illusions for Joao. And he wondered if this were the *tranquility* referred to in the song.

A flock of tanagers caught his attention. They swept overhead, glistening turquoise, dived into the jungle wall and were swallowed by it as though they'd never been.

The mango shore on the left gave way to a narrow strip of grass on a medium embankment, red-brown earth pitted with holes.

The hatch opened, and Joao heard Chen-Lhu clamber into the cabin. There came the sound of the hatch being closed and dogged.

"Johnny, do I see something moving in the trees behind that grass?" Chen-Lhu asked.

Joao focused his attention on the scene. *Yes!* Something just inside the tree shadows—many figures that moved like a flitting current to keep pace with the pod.

Joao lifted the sprayrifle which he had wedged to the left of his seat.

"That's a long shot," Rhin said.

"I know. I just want to put them on notice—keep them at a distance."

He fumbled with the seal on the gunport, but before he could open it, the figures stepped out of the shadows into the full sunlight of the grassy beach.

Joao gasped.

"Mother of God, Mother of God. . . ." Rhin whispered.

It was a mixed group standing as though on review along the shore. They were mostly human in shape, although there were a few giant copies of insect forms—mantidae, beetles, something with a whiplike proboscis. The humans were mainly in the form of Indians and most of those like the ones who'd kidnapped Joao and his father.

Interspersed along the line, though, stood single editions, individuals: there, one identical in appearance to the Prefect, Joao's father; beside him . . . Vierho! and all the men from the camp.

Joao pushed the sprayrifle through the port.

"No!" Rhin said. "Wait. See their eyes, how glassy they look. Those could be our friends . . . drugged or . . ." She broke off.

Or worse, Joao thought.

"It's possible they're hostages," Chen-Lhu said, "One sure way to find out—shoot one of them." He stood up, opened the gig-box. "Here's a hard-pellet . . ."

"Stuff that!" Joao snarled. He withdrew his sprayrifle, sealed the port.

Chen-Lhu pursed his lips in thought. *These Latins! So unrealistic.* He returned the hard-pellet rifle to the box, sat down. One of the lesser individuals could have been chosen as target. Valuable information could have been gained. Pressing the issue now would gain nothing, though. Not now.

"I don't know about you two," Rhin said, "but in my school we were taught not to kill our friends."

"Of course, Rhin, of course," Chen-Lhu said. "But are those our friends?"

She said, "Until I know for sure . . ."

"Exactly!" Chen-Lhu said. "And how will you know for sure?" He pointed toward the figures standing now behind them as the shore once more drifted into a line of overhanging trees and vines. "That is a school, too, Rhin—that jungle over there. You should learn its lesson, too."

Double meaning, double meaning, she thought.

"The jungle is a school of pragmatism," Chen-Lhu said. "Absolute judgments. Ask it about good and evil? The jungle has one answer: *'That which succeeds is good.'* "

He's telling me to get on with the seduction of Senhor Johnny Martinho while the poor fool's still wide open from shock, she thought. *True enough—danger, shock and horror, they all create their own rebound.*

She nodded to herself. *But where do I bounce?*

"If those were Indians, I'd know why they put on that show," Joao said. "But those are not really Indians. We cannot tell how these creatures think. Indians would do that sort of thing to taunt us, saying: 'You're next.' But these creatures . . ." He shook his head.

Silence invaded the pod: an impressive solitude magnified by heat and the hypnotic flow of shoreline.

Chen-Lhu lay back, drowsing, thought: *I will let the heat and idleness do my work for me.*

Joao stared at his hands.

He'd never before been trapped in a situation where both fear and idleness forced him to look inward. The experience terrified and fascinated him.

Fear is the penalty of consciousness forced to stare at itself, Joao thought. *I should be busy with something. With what? Sleep, then.*

But he feared sleep because he sensed dreams poised there.

Emptiness . . . what a prize that would be: emptiness, he thought.

He felt that somewhere in his past he had reached a glowing summit devoid of before-and-after complications, a place of no doubts. Action . . . play . . . reflex motion—that had been the life. Now, it all lay there, open to introspection, open to study and re-examination.

But he sensed there might be a tip-over point with introspection, that somewhere within him lurked memories which could engulf him.

Rhin rested her head against the back of the seat, looked up at the sky. *Someone'll start looking for us soon*, she thought. *They must . . . they must . . . they must.*

Must rhymes with lust, she thought. And she swallowed, wondering where that thought had originated. She forced her attention onto the sky—so blue . . . blue . . . blue: a blank surface upon which anything could be written.

Searchers could come over us at any minute now.

Her gaze wavered, went to the mountains along the western horizon. Mountains grew and diminished there as the river carried her through its blue furrow.

It's the things we must not think about because they'd overpower us with emotion, she thought. *These things are the terrible burden.* Her hand crept out, clasped Joao's. He didn't look at her, but the pressure of his response was more than a hand enfolding hers.

Chen-Lhu saw the motion and smiled.

Joao stared out at the passing shore. The pod drifted on an enchanted current between drooping curtains of lianas. The current carried them around a bend, exposing the towered brilliance of three *Fernan Sanchez* trees: imperative red against the green. But Joao's eye went to the water where the river was at work, slowly undercutting clawed roots in the muddy bank.

Her hand in mine, he thought. *Her hand in mine.*

Her palm was moist, intimate, possessive.

Rising waves of heat encased the pod in dead air. The sun grew to a throbbing inferno that drifted over them . . . slowly, slowly settling toward the western peaks.

Hands together . . . hands together, Joao thought.

He began to pray for the night.

Evening shadows began to quilt the river's edges. Night swept upward from the trench of slow current toward the blazing peaks.

Chen-Lhu stirred, sat up as the sun dipped behind the mountains. Amethyst vapors from the sunset produced a space of polished ruby water ahead of the pod—like flowing blood. There came a moment at the dark when the river appeared to cease all movement. Then they entered the damply cushioned night.

This is the time of the timid and the terrible, Chen-Lhu thought. *The night is my time—and I am not timid.*

And he smiled at the way the two shadows in the front seats had become one shadow.

The animal with two backs, he thought. It was such

an amusing thought that he put a hand to his mouth to suppress laughter.

Presently, Chen-Lhu spoke: "I will sleep now, Johnny. You take the first watch. Wake me at midnight."

The small stirring noises from the front of the cabin ceased momentarily, then resumed.

"Right," Joao said, and his voice was husky.

Ahh, that Rhin, Chen-Lhu thought. *Such a good tool even when she does not want to be.*

8

The report, although interesting for its variations, added little to the Brain's general information about humans. They reacted with shock and fear to the display along the river bank. That was to be expected. The Chinese had demonstrated practicality not shared by the other two. This fact, added to the apparent attempts of the Chinese to get the other two to mate— that might be significant. Time would tell.

Meanwhile, the Brain experienced something akin to another human emotion—worry.

The trio in the vehicle were drifting farther and farther away from the chamber above the river chasm. A significant delay factor was entering the system of report-computation-decision-action.

The Brain's sensors reviewed once more the messenger pattern being repeated on the cavern ceiling.

The vehicle was approaching a series of rapids. Its occupants could be killed there and irrevocably lost. Or they might renew their efforts to fly away in the craft.

There lay a worry-element requiring a heavy weighing factor.

The vehicle had flown once.

Computation-decision.

"You report to the action groups," the Brain commanded. "Tell them to capture the vehicle and occupants before they reach the rapids. Capture the humans alive, if possible. Order of importance if some of them must be sacrificed: first the Chinese is to be taken, then the dormant queen, and finally the other male."

The insects on the ceiling danced their message pattern and hummed the modulation elements to fix them, then took off into the dawnlight at the cavemouth.

Action.

Chen-Lhu stared downriver across the front seats, watching the moonpath crawl beneath the pod. The path rippled with spider lines in the eddies, flowed like painted silk in the broad reaches.

The breathing sounds of deep, satiated sleep came from the front of the cabin.

Now I probably will not have to kill that fool, Johnny, Chen-Lhu thought.

He looked out the side windows at the moon, low and near to setting. Bronze earthlight filled out the hiddle circle. Within this darker area there appeared the likeness of a face: Vierho.

He is dead, Johnny's companion, Chen-Lhu thought. *That was a simulacrum we saw beside the river. Nothing could've survived that attack on the camp. Our friends out there have copied dear Padre.*

Chen-Lhu asked himself then: *I wonder how Vierho encountered death—as an illusion or as a cataclysm?*

A bootless question.

Rhin turned in her sleep, pressed close to Joao. "Mmmmm," she murmured.

Our friends will not hold off the attack much longer, Chen-Lhu thought. *It's obvious they've just been awaiting the proper time and place. Where will it come—in a rock-filled gorge, at a narrow place? Where?*

The thought turned every shadow outside into a source of peril, and Chen-Lhu wondered at himself that he could have allowed his mind to play such a fear-inspiring trick.

Still, he strained his senses against the night.

There *was* a waiting-silence outside, a feeling of presence in the jungle.

This is nonsense! Chen-Lhu told himself.

He cleared his throat.

Joao turned against the seat, felt Rhin's head cradled against him. How quietly she breathed.

"Travis," he whispered.

"Yes?"

"Time's it?"

"Go back to sleep, Johnny. You've a couple more hours."

Joao closed his eyes, lay back into his seat, but deep sleep evaded him. Something about the cabin . . . something. There was something here demanding his recognition. His awareness came farther and farther out of sleep.

Mildew.

It was stronger in the cabin than it had been—and there was the acrid tang of rust.

The smells filled Joao with melancholy. He could feel the pod deteriorating around him, and the pod was a symbol of civilization. These imperative odors represented all human decay and mortality.

He stroked Rhin's hair, thought: *Why shouldn't we*

grab a little happiness here, now? Tomorrow we could be dead ... or worse.

Slowly, he sank back into sleep.

A flock of parakeets announced the dawn. They chattered and gossiped in the jungle beside the river. Smaller birds joined the chorus—flutterings, chirps, twitters.

Joao heard the birds as though from an enormous distance pulling him upward to wakefulness. He awoke, sweating, feeling oddly weak.

Rhin had moved away from him in the night. She slept curled against her side of the cabin.

Joao stared out at blue-white light. Smoky mist hid the river upstream and downstream. There was a feeling of moist, unhealthy warmth in the closed cabin's air. His mouth tasted dry and bitter.

He sat up straight, leaned forward to look through the overhead curve of windshield. His back ached from sleeping in a cramped position.

"Don't look up for searchers, Johnny," Chen-Lhu said.

Joao coughed, said, "I was just looking at the weather. We're going to get rain soon."

"Perhaps."

So gray, that sky, Joao thought. It was an empty slate prepared as a setting for one vulture that sailed into view across the treetops, wings motionless. The vulture tipped majestically, beat its wings once ... twice ... and flew upstream.

Joao lowered his gaze, noted that the pod had become part of a drifting island of logs and brush during the night. He could see parasite moss on the logs. It was an old island—at least one season old ... no, older. The moss was thick.

As he watched, an eddy came between the pod and the logs. They parted company.

"Where are we?" Rhin asked.

Joao turned to see her sitting up, awake. She avoided his eyes.

What the hell? he thought. *Is she ashamed?*

"We are where we've always been, my dear Rhin," Chen-Lhu said. "We're on the river. Are you hungry?"

She considered the question, found that she was ravenous.

"Yes, I'm hungry."

They ate in quick silence with Joao growing more and more convinced that Rhin was avoiding him. She was first out the hatch to the float and stayed a long time. When she returned, she lay back in the seat, pretending sleep.

To hell with her, Joao thought. He went out the hatch, slammed it after him.

Chen-Lhu leaned forward, whispered close to Rhin's ear, "You were very good last night, my dear."

She spoke without opening her eyes: "To hell with you."

"But I don't believe in hell."

"And I do?" She opened her eyes, stared at him.

"Of course."

"Each in his own way," she said, and she closed her eyes.

For some reason he couldn't explain, her words and action angered him, and he tried to goad her with what he knew of her beliefs: "You are a terrible aboriginal calamity!"

Again, she spoke without opening her eyes: "That's Cardinal Newman. Stuff Cardinal Newman."

"You don't believe in original sin?" he jeered.

"I only believe in certain kinds of hell," she said, and

again she was looking at him, the green eyes steady.

"To each his own, eh?"

"You said it; I didn't."

"But you did say it."

"Is that right?"

"Yes! You said it!"

"You're shouting," she said.

He took a moment to calm himself, then, in a whisper: "And Johnny, was he good?"

"Better than you could ever be."

Joao opened the hatch and entered the cabin before Chen-Lhu could answer, found Rhin staring up at him.

"Howdy, Jefe," she said. And she smiled, a warm, intimate, sharing smile.

Joao answered the smile, slipped into his seat. "We're going to hit rapids today," he said. "I can feel it. What were you shouting about, Travis?"

"It was nothing," Chen-Lhu said, but his voice still grated with anger.

"It was an ideological issue," Rhin said. "Travis remains a militant atheist to the end. Me, I believe in heaven." She stroked Joao's cheek.

"Why do you think we are near rapids?" Chen-Lhu asked. And he thought: *I must divert this conversation! This is a dangerous game you play with me, Rhin.*

"Current's faster, for one thing," Joao said.

He stared out the front windows. A new, surging character definitely had come over the river. Hills had drawn closer to the channel. More eddies trailed their lines from the shores.

A band of long-tailed monkeys began pacing the pod. They roared and chittered through the trees along the left bank, only to abandon the game at a river bend.

"Every creature I see out there, I have to ask myself: Is that really what it seems?" Rhin said.

"Those are really monkeys," Joao said. "I think there are some things our friends cannot imitate."

The river straightened now, and the hills pressed closer. Thick twistings of hardwood trees along both shores gave way to lines of sago palms backed by rising waves of the jungle's omnipresent greens. Only infrequently was the green broken by smooth red-skinned trunks of *guayavilla* leaning over the water.

Around another bend, and they surprised a long-legged pink bird feeding in the shallows. It lifted on heavy pinions, flew downstream.

"Fasten your seatbelts," Joao said.

"Are you that certain?" Chen-Lhu asked.

"Yes."

Joao heard buckles snapping, fastened his own harness, looked at the dash to review Vierho's changes in controls. Igniter . . . firing light . . . throttle. He moved the wheel; how sluggish it felt. One silent prayer for the patch on the right hand float, and he set himself in readiness.

The sound came as a faint roaring like wind through trees. They felt another quickening of the current that swept the pod around a wide bend, turning in an eddy until it faced directly downstream, and there, no more than a kilometer away, they saw the snarled boiling of white water. Foam and misting spume hurled itself into the air. The sound was a crashing drum roar growing louder by the second.

Joao weighed the circumstances—high walls of trees on both sides, narrowing channel, high black walls of wet rock on both sides of the rapids. There was only one way to go: through it.

Current and distance required careful judgment: the pod's floats had to hit the crosscurrent waves above the rapids at just the right moment for those waves to help break the river's grip on the floats.

This'll be the place, Chen-Lhu thought. *Our friends'll be here . . . waiting for us*. He gripped a sprayrifle, tried to see both shores at once.

Rhin gripped the sides of her seat, pressed herself backward against the cushions. She felt that they were hurtling without hope toward the maelstrom.

"Something in the trees on our right," Chen-Lhu said. "Something overhead."

A shadow darkened the water all around them. Fluttering white shapes began to obscure the view ahead.

Joao punched the igniter, counted—one, two, three. Light off—throttle.

The motors caught with a great banging, spitting roar that drowned the sound of the rapids. The pod surged through the screen of insects, out of the shadow. Joao swerved them to avoid a line of foaming rocks in the upper pool. He nursed the throttle by the feeling of G-pressure against his back.

Don't blow, baby, he prayed. *Don't blow*.

"A net!" Rhin screamed. "They have a net across the river!"

It lifted from the water above the rapids like a dripping snake.

Reflex moved Joao's hand on the throttle, sent the knob slamming against the dash.

The pod leaped, skimmed across a glossy pool. Slithering current tugged them sideways toward smooth black walls of rock. The net stood out directly ahead when the pod lifted, floats breaking from the water.

Up . . . up.

Joao could see the river plunge off beyond the net, water leaping in crazy violence there as though trying to escape the glassy black walls of rock.

Something slapped the floats with a screech and sound of tearing. The pod's nose dipped, bounced up as Joao hauled on the wheel. A staccato rattling shook the craft. Spray filled the air all around.

In one flickering moment, Joao saw motion along the chasm's rim. A line of boulders thundered down there, fell behind.

Then they were out of it, airborne and climbing-lurching-twisting . . . but climbing. Joao eased the throttle back.

The pod thundered over a line of trees, back across the river. Another tree-spiked hill shot beneath them. A long straight avenue of water opened out ahead of them like turbulent brown grease.

Joao grew conscious of Rhin's voice: "Look at us go! Look at us go!

"That was inspired flying," Chen-Lhu said.

Joao tried to swallow in a dry throat. The controls felt heavy under his hands. He saw downstream a great bend in the river, and beyond that a wide island-broken lake of flooded land.

Brown river . . . flooded land, he thought.

He fishtailed the pod, shot a look back to the west. Brown clouds were piled there, with black beneath them: thunderheads! *Rain in the hills behind us*, he thought. *Flood here. It must've happened during the night*.

And he cursed himself for not noticing the change in water color earlier.

"What's wrong, Johnny?" Chen-Lhu asked.

"Nothing we can do anything about."

Joao eased the throttle back another notch, another. The motors sputtered, died. He shut off all fuel.

Wind whistled around them as Joao eased back on the wheel, trying to gain as much distance as possible.

The pod began to stagger at the edge of stalling. He tipped the nose down, still nursing it for distance. But the pod flew like all pods—gliding like a rock.

The wind of their passage was an eerie whistling that filled the cabin.

The river curved off to the left through more drowned land. A thin furrow of turbulent water marked the main channel. Gently, Joao banked the pod, turned to follow that furrow. The water rushed up to meet them. The pod began to yaw and Joao fought the controls.

Floats touched in a splashing, rocking motion with too much drag. An eddy turned the pod. The right wing began to drop—lower, lower.

Joao aimed for a brown sand beach on their left.

"We're sinking," Rhin said, and her voice conveyed both surprise and horror in a flat tone of understatement.

"That right float," Chen-Lhu said. "I felt it hit the net."

The left float grated on sand, stopped, spun the sinking float in a short arc until it, too, touched. Something gurgled under the water to the right and a burst of bubbles lifted to the surface. Less than six millimeters of air remained between the right wing tip and the water.

Rhin buried her head in her hands and shuddered.

"Now what?" Chen-Lhu asked. And he felt shocked amusement as he heard the dismay in his own voice.

Now it is the end, he thought. *Our friends will find us here. It is the end for sure.*

"Now we repair the float," Joao said.

Rhin lifted her face from her hands, stared at him.

"Out here?" Chen-Lhu asked. "Ahhh, Johnny. . . ."

Rhin pressed the back of her left hand against her mouth, thought: *Joao—he just said that to keep me from despair.*

"Certainly, out here!" Joao snapped. "Now shut up while I think."

Rhin lowered her hand, said, "Is it possible?"

"If they give us enough time," Joao said.

He broke the canopy seals, folded it forward. The sound of brawling water impressed itself on his senses. He unfastened his safety harness, all the while looking around, studying the air, the jungle, the river.

No insects.

Joao climbed out, slipped down to the slanted surface of the left float, studied the jungle beyond the beach: a confusion of interlaced branches, vines, creepers and tree ferns.

"There could be an army just inside that jungle and we couldn't see them," Chen-Lhu whispered.

Joao looked up. The Chinese stood at the inner edge of the cabin.

"How do you propose to repair the float?" Chen-Lhu asked.

Rhin appeared beside him, waited for the answer.

"I don't know yet," Joao said. He turned, looked downstream. A line of ripples moved up the river there, pushed by a wind out of a furnace. The ripples fanned out before the wind and grew as the wind grew. Then the wind died. Air and water wavered in the damp heat. A pressure of heat radiated from the pod's metal and from the beach.

Joao slid off into the water. It felt warm and thick.

"What about the cannibal fish?" Rhin asked.

"They can't see me; I can't see them," Joao said. "A fair exchange."

He splashed around beneath the rocket motors. The smell of unburned fuel was strong there and an oily glaze of it was beginning to trail off downstream. Joao shrugged, bent and ran a hand gently along the outer edge of the right float, wading forward as he explored the hidden surface.

Just back of the leading edge, his fingers encountered a jagged rip in the metal and trailing remnants of Vierho's patch. Joao explored the hole. It was a dismayingly big one.

Metal scraped as Chen-Lhu dropped down to the left float, a sprayrifle in his hand. "How bad is it?" he asked.

Joao straightened, waded out to the beach. "Bad enough."

"Well, can it be fixed?" Chen-Lhu demanded.

Joao turned, looked at the man, surprised by the grating quality in Chen-Lhu's voice.

He's frightened silly! Joao thought.

"We'll have to get that float out of the water before I can be sure," Joao said. "But I think we can patch it."

"How'll you get it out of the water?"

"Vines . . . a Spanish windlass, limbs for rollers."

Rhin spoke from the cabin: "How long?"

"By tonight, if we're lucky," Joao said.

"They won't give us that long," Chen-Lhu said.

"We gained thirty or forty kilometers on them," Joao said.

"But they, too, can fly," Chen-Lhu said. He raised the sprayrifle, aiming upstream. "And here they come."

Joao whirled as Chen-Lhu fired, was in time to see a broad front of spraybursts knock down a fluttering line of white, red and gold insects, each as long as a man's thumb. But more came behind . . . and more . . . and more. . . .

"And again it flew," the Brain accused.

The messengers on the ceiling danced and hummed their report, made way for a new group flitting in like bits of golden mica through the sunlight at the cave-mouth.

"The vehicle is down and badly damaged," the new-comers reported. "It no longer floats on the water, but lies partly beneath the water. The humans do not appear to be damaged. We already are leading the action groups to the place, but the humans are shooting their poisons at everything that moves. What are your in-structions?"

The Brain worked to quiet itself for computation and decision. *Emotions . . . emotions*, it thought. *Emotions are the curse of logic.*

Data-data-data—it was loaded with data. But always there was that shading-off factor. New events modified old facts. The Brain knew many facts about humans—observational facts, some achieved deductively and in-ductively, some garnered from microfilms libraries the humans had stored in the Red against the time of their return.

So many gaps in the data.

The Brain longed then for the ability to move about by itself, to observe with its own sensors what it could only gather from messengers now. The wish brought a rash of fuzzy signals from the dormant and almost at-rophied muscle-control centers. Nurse insects scurried over the Brain's surface, feeding where these unusual demands arose, countering with hormonal additives the frustration blockages that for a moment threatened the entire structure.

Atheism, the Brain thought, as chemical serenity re-turned. *They spoke of atheism and heaven* (*religion-subtended*). These matters puzzled the Brain. The conversation, reportedly, had come out of an argument and pertained somehow to the human mating pattern . . . at least among the humans in the vehicle.

The insects on the ceiling jittered through a repetition of their message. "What are your instructions?"

What are my instructions?

My instructions.

I . . . me . . . my.

Again, the nurse insects scurried.

Calmness returned to the Brain, and it wondered at the fact that thoughts—mere thoughts—could bring such upset. The same thing appeared to occur with humans.

"The humans in the vehicle must be captured alive," the Brain commanded. (And it realized the command was a selfish one. It had so many questions for this trio.) "Take in all available action groups. Locate a suitable place downriver, better than the last one, and post half the action groups there. The other half must attack as soon as possible."

The brain subsided without releasing its messengers, then, almost as an afterthought: "If all else fails, kill everything except their heads. Save and maintain their heads."

Now, the messengers were released. They had their instructions, and they fluttered out of the cave into the bright sunlight above the roar of water.

In the west, a cloud passed over the sun.

And the Brain marked this fact, noting that the sound of the river was louder today.

Rains in the highlands, it thought. This thought elicited images within its memory: wet leaves, rivulets on the forest floor, damp cold air, feet splashing on gray clay.

The feet of the image appeared to be its own, and the Brain found this an odd fact. But the nurse insects had the chemical serenity of their charge well in hand now, and the Brain went on to consider every datum it possessed about Cardinal Newman. Nowhere could it discover reference to a *stuffed* Cardinal Newman.

The patch consisted of leaves bound with tent lines and vines on the outside and spray coagulant from a doctored foamal bomb which Joao had exploded inside the float. The pod floated upright on the river beside the beach now while he stood waist deep beside it, checking their work.

The charged hiss and cork-popping of sprayrifles and foamal bombs went on intermittently above him. The air was thick with the bitter smell of the poisons. Black and orange scum floated past him down the river and lay in puff mounds on the beach around the remains of their vine-powered windlass. Each bit of scum carried its imbedded collection of dead and dying insects.

Rhin leaned over during a lull in the attack, said, "For the love of God, how much longer?"

"It seems to be holding," Joao rasped.

He rubbed at his neck and arms. Not all the insects were being caught by the sprayrifles and bombs. His skin felt like fire from the accumulation of stings and bites. When he looked up at Rhin, he saw that her forehead was welted.

"If it's holding, shove us off," Chen-Lhu said. He appeared above Joao, standing beside Rhin, glanced down and returned his attention to the sky.

Joao staggered with a sudden dizziness, almost fell. His body ached with weariness. It required a distinct effort to lift his head and scan the sky around them. Distant sky. They had perhaps an hour of daylight left.

"For God's sake, shove off!" Rhin shouted.

Joao grew aware that the firing had resumed. He pulled himself along the float toward the beach, and the action sent the pod outward. It swung over him and he stared stupidly upward at the patched belly tank wondering who had done that work.

Oh, yes—Vierho.

The pod continued to drift outward, caught now by the current. It was at least two meters from Joao when he realized he was supposed to be aboard it. He lunged for the right float, caught its rear edge and hauled himself sprawling onto it with almost the last of his strength.

A hand reached down from the open hatch, grabbed his collar. With the help of the hand, he clambered to his knees, crawled up into the cabin. Only when he was inside did he see that it was Rhin's hand.

They had the canopy down and sealed, he noted.

Chen-Lhu was darting around the interior smashing insects with a roll of charts.

Joao felt something sting his right leg, looked down to see Rhin kneeling there and applying a fresh energy-pack.

Why is she doing that? he wondered. Then he remembered: *Oh, yes—the stings, the poisons.*

"Won't we have some immunity from the last bout?" he asked and was surprised when his voice came out a whisper.

"Maybe," she said. "Unless they hit us with something new."

"I think I have most of them," Chen-Lhu said. "Rhin, did you seal the hatch?"

"Yes."

"I sprayed with the hand unit under the seats and dash." Chen-Lhu reached down, put a hand under Joao's arm. "Here we go, Johnny. Into your seat, eh?"

"Yes." Joao staggered forward, sank into the seat. His head felt as though it rested on slack rubber. "Are we in the current?" he gasped.

"We seem to be," Chen-Lhu said.

Joao sat there panting. He could feel the energy pack like a distant army working inward against his weariness. Perspiration flooded his skin, but his mouth felt dry and hot. The windshield ahead of him was dappled with the orange and black spray and foam residue.

"They're still with us," Chen-Lhu said. "Along the shore over there and some kind of a group overhead."

Joao peered around him. Rhin had returned to her seat. She sat with a sprayrifle across her lap, her head thrown back, eyes closed. Chen-Lhu knelt on the gigbox and peered at the left-hand shore.

The interior of the cabin appeared to Joao to be filled with dappled gray-green shadows. His mind told him there must be other colors present, but he saw only the gray-green—even Chen-Lhu's skin . . . and Rhin's.

"Something's . . . wrong . . . with . . . color," he whispered.

"Color aberration," Chen-Lhu said. "That was one of the symptoms."

Joao looked out a clear place in the right windows, saw through the trees a scattering of dun peaks and a gray-green sun low above them.

"Close your eyes, lean back and relax," Rhin said.

Joao rolled his head on the seat back, saw that she had put aside her sprayrifle and was bending over him. She began massaging his forehead.

She spoke to Chen-Lhu: "His skin feels hot."

Joao closed his eyes. Her hands felt so peaceful and cool. The blackness of utter fatigue hovered around him . . . and far off on his right leg he felt a drumbeat: the energy pack.

"Try to sleep," Rhin whispered.

"Rhin, how do you feel?" Chen-Lhu asked.

"I put a pack on my leg during that first lull," she

said. "I think it's the ACTH fractions—they seem to give immediate relief if you haven't been hit too hard."

"And Johnny got much more than we did from our friends."

"Out there? Of course he did."

The word sounds were a distant fuzziness to Joao, but the meanings rang through with a startling clarity, and he found himself fascinated by voice overtones. Chen-Lhu's voice was loaded with concealment. Rhin's carried suppressed fear and genuine concern for himself.

Rhin gave his forehead one last soothing caress, sank back into her seat. She pushed her hair back, looked out to the west. Movement there, yes: white flutterings and things that were larger. She moved her gaze upward. Alto cirrus clouds hung in the distance above the trees. Sunset poured color through them as she watched and the clouds became waves as red as blood.

She averted her eyes, looked downstream.

The current swept the pod around a sickle-shaped bend and they drifted almost due north in a widening channel. Along the eastern shore the water flowed with mauve-tinted silver, metallic and luminous.

A deep booming of jungle doves sounded from the right bank—or was it doves. Rhin looked around her, feeling the hushed stillness.

The sun dipped behind distant peaks and the nightly patrol of bats flickered overhead, swooping and soaring. Noises of evening birds lifted, stilled and were replaced by night sounds—the far off coughing growl of a jaguar, rustlings and quiverings and a nearby splash.

And again that hushed stillness.

Something out there that everything in the jungle fears, Rhin thought.

An amber moon began to climb over them. The pod drifted down the moonpath like a giant dragonfly poised on the water. A skeleton butterfly fluttered into view through the pale light, waved the filigree of its transparent wings on the pod's windshield, departed.

"They're keeping a close watch on us," Chen-Lhu said.

Joao could feel warmth coursing upward from the energy pack as the ATP, the calcium and acetylcholine, the ACTH ractions diffused in his body. But a sensation of dizziness remained, as though he were many persons at once. He opened his eyes, looked out to the fuzzy spread of moonlit hills. He realized he actually saw this, but part of him felt as though it clung to the fabric ceiling of the cabin behind the canopy, crouching there, really. And the moon was an alien moon, like none he had ever known, its earth-lighted circle far too big, its melon-curve of sun reflection far too bright. It was a false moon on a painted backdrop and it made him feel small, dwindling away to a tiny spark lost in the infinity of the universe.

He pressed his eyes tightly closed, berating himself: *I mustn't think like that or I'll go crazy! God! What's wrong with me?*

Joao felt that a pressure of silence filled the cabin. He strained to hear tiny sounds—Rhin's controlled breathing. Chen-Lhu clearing his throat.

Good and evil are man-made opposites: there is only honor. Joao heard the thought as words echoing in his mind and recognized them. Those were his father's words . . . his father, now dead and become a simulacrum to haunt him by standing beside the river.

Men anchor their lives at a station between good and evil.

"You know, Rhin, this is a Marxian river," Chen-Lhu said. "Everything in the universe flows like this river. Everything changes constantly from one form to another. Dialectic. Nothing can stop this; nothing *should* stop this. Nothing's static, nothing ever twice the same."

"Oh, shut up," Rhin muttered.

"You western women," Chen-Lhu said. "You don't understand dialectical reality."

"Tell it to the bugs," she said.

"How rich this land is," Chen-Lhu murmured. "How very rich. Do you have any idea of how many of *my* people this land could support. With only the slightest alteration—clearings, terraces . . . In China, we've learned how to make such land support millions of people."

Rhin sat up, stared across the seat back at Chen-Lhu. "How's that again?"

"These stupid Brazilians, they never learned how to use this land. But *my* people . . ."

"I see. Your people come in here and show them how, is that it?"

"It is a possibility," Chen-Lhu said, and he thought: *Digest that for a bit, my dear Rhin. When you see how great the the prize, you will understand the price that might be paid.*

"And what about the Brazilians—quite a few million of them—who're crowded into the cities and the farm plots of the Resettlement Plan while their Ecological Realignment is progressing?"

"They are becoming used to their present condition."

"They can stand it only because they have hopes for something better!"

"Ah, no, my dear Rhin, you don't understand people very well. Governments can manipulate people to gain anything that's found necessary."

"And what about the insects?" she asked. "What about the Great Crusade?"

Chen-Lhu shrugged. "We lived with them for thousands of years . . . before."

"And the mutations, the new species?"

"Yes, the creations of your bandeirante friends—those we very likely will have to destroy."

"I'm not so sure the bandeirantes created those . . . things out there," she said. "I'm sure Joao had nothing to do with it."

"Ah . . . then who did?"

"Perhaps the same people who don't want to admit their own Great Crusade's failure!"

Chen-Lhu put down anger, said, "I tell you it is not true."

She looked down at Joao breathing so deeply, obviously asleep. Was it possible? No!

Chen-Lhu sat back, thinking: *Let her consider these things. Doubt is all I need and she will serve me most usefully, my lovely little tool. And Johnny Martinho—what a lovely scapegoat: trained in North America, an unprincipled tool of the imperialists! A man of no shame, who made love to one of my own people right in front of me. His fellows will believe such a man capable of anything!*

A quiet smile moved Chen-Lhu's lips.

Rhin, looking into the rear of the cabin, could see only the harsh angular features of the IEO chief. *He's so strong*, she thought. *And I'm so tired.*

She lowered her head onto Joao's lap like a child seeking comfort, burrowed her left hand behind his back. How feverishly warm he felt. Her burrowing hand encountered a bulky metallic shape in Joao's jacket. She explored the outline with her fingers, recognized it as a gun . . . a hand weapon.

Rhin withdrew her hand, sat up. *Why does he carry a weapon which he conceals from us?*

Joao continued to breath deeply, feigning sleep. Chen-Lhu's words screamed through his mind, warning him, urging him to action. But caution intervened.

Rhin stared downstream wondering . . . doubting. The pod floated down a lane of moon glitter. Cold glows like fireflies danced in the forest darkness on both sides. A feeling of corruption came to her from that darkness.

Joao, reflecting on Chen-Lhu's words, thought: *"Everything in the universe flows like a river."* Why do I hesitate? I could turn and kill the bastard . . . or force him to tell the truth about himself. What part does Rhin play in this? She sounded angry with him "Everything in the universe flows like a river."*

Introspection came hard to Joao, bringing dread, inner trembling that moved toward terror. *Those creatures out there*, he thought, *time is on their side. My life is like a river. I flow—moments, memories . . . nothing eternal, no absolutes.*

He felt feverish, dizzy and his own heartbeat intruded on his awareness.

Like a river.

He's not going to warn anyone about the debacle in China. He has a plan . . . something in which he wants to use me.

The night wind had grown stronger and now it imparted an uneasy shifting motion to the pod, catching first one stubwing and then the other. As it came through the vent filters, a damp nutrient in the wind fed Joao's awareness. He moaned as though awakening, sat up.

Rhin touched his arm. "How are you?" There was concern in her voice, and something else Joao could not recognize. Withdrawal? Shame?

"I . . . so warm," he whispered.

"Water," she said, and lifted a canteen to his lips.

The water felt cool, although he knew it must be warm. Part of it ran down his jaw and he realized then how weak he was in spite of the energy pack The effort of swallowing required a terrible energy drain.

I'm sick, he thought. *I'm really sick . . . very sick.*

He allowed his head to fall against the back of the seat, stared up through the canopy's transparent strip. The stars intruded on his awareness—sharp specks of light that stabbed through rushing clouds. The fitful wind-swayed motion of the pod sent stars and clouds tipping across his field of vision. The sensation began to make him feel nauseated, and he lowered his gaze, saw the flitting lights on the right shore.

"Travis," he whispered.

"Heh?" And Chen-Lhu wondered how long Joao had been awake. *Was I fooled by his breathing? Did I say too much?*

"Lights," Joao said. "Over there . . . lights."

"Oh. Those. They've been with us for quite awhile. Our friends out there are keeping track of us."

"How wide's the river here?" Rhin asked.

"A hundred meters or so," Chen-Lhu said.

"How can they see us?"

"How can they not in this moonlight?"

"Shouldn't I give them a shot just to . . ."

"Save the ammunition," Chen-Lhu said. "After that mess today . . . well, we couldn't stand off another such day."

"I hear something," Rhin said. "Is it rapids?"

Joao pushed himself upright. The effort it required terrified him. *I couldn't handle the controls like this,* he thought. *And I doubt if Rhin or Travis know how.*

He grew aware of a hissing sound.

"What is that?" Chen-Lhu asked.

Joao sighed, sank back. "Shallows, something in the river. Off there to the left." The sound grew louder: the rhythmic lament of water against a stranded limb—and faded behind them.

"What'd happen if that right float hit something like that?" Rhin asked.

"End of the ride," Joao said.

An eddy turned the pod, began sawing it back and forth in a slow, persistent pendulum—around, back, around. . . . The floats danced across ripples and the pendulum stopped.

The darkly flowing jungle, the lights sent waves of drowsiness through Joao. He knew he could not stay awake if his life depended on it.

"I'll stand a watch tonight, Travis," Rhin said.

"I wonder why our friends out there don't bother us much at night?" Chen-Lhu said. "It's very curious."

"They're not losing sight of us, though," Rhin said. "Go to sleep. I'll take the first watch."

"Watch and nothing else," Chen-Lhu said.

"What's that supposed to mean?"

"Just don't go to sleep, my dear Rhin."

"Go to hell," she said.

"You forget: I don't believe in hell."

Joao awoke to the sound of rain and darkness that slowly crept into gray dawn. The light increased until he could see steel lines of downpour slanting against pale green jungle on his left. The other shore was a distant gray. It was a rain of monotonous violence that drummed against the canopy and pocked the river with countless tiny craters.

"Are you awake?" Rhin asked.

Joao sat up, found he felt refreshed and curiously clear headed. "How long's it been raining like this?"

"Since about midnight."

Chen-Lhu cleared his throat, leaned forward close to

Joao. "I've seen no sign of our friends for hours. Could it be they don't like rain?"

"I don't like rain," Joao said.

"What do you mean?" Rhin asked.

"This river's going to become a raging hell."

Joao looked up to his left at clouds hovering low above the trees. "And if there ever were going to be searchers, they sure as hell couldn't see us now."

Rhin wet her lips with her tongue. She felt suddenly emptied of emotion, realized then how much she had counted on being found. "How . . . how long does the rain last?" she asked.

"Four or five months," Joao said.

An eddy turned the pod. Shoreline twisted across Joao's vision: greenery dimmed to pastel by the torrent. "Anybody been outside?" he asked.

"I have," Chen-Lhu said.

Joao turned, saw dark patches of wetness on the IEO fatigues.

"Nothing out there except rain," Chen-Lhu said.

Joao's right leg began to itch. He reached down, was surprised to find the energy pack gone.

"You began showing muscle spasms during the night," Rhin said. "I took it off."

"I must've really been asleep." He touched her hand. "Thanks, nurse."

She pulled her hand away.

Joao looked up, puzzled, but she turned, stared out her window.

"I'm . . . going outside," Joao said.

"Do you feel strong enough?" she asked. "You were pretty weak."

"I'm all right."

He stood up, made his way back to the hatch and down to the pontoon. The rain felt warm and fresh against his face. He stood on the end of the float, enjoying the freshness.

In the cabin, Chen-Lhu said, "Why didn't you go out and hold his hand, Rhin?"

"You're an utter bastard, Travis," she said.

"Do you love him a little?"

She turned, glared at him. "What do you want from me?"

"Your cooperation, my dear."

"In what?"

"How would you like to have an emerald mine all your very own? Or perhaps diamonds? More wealth than you could possibly imagine?"

"In payment for what?"

"When the moment comes, Rhin, you'll know what to do. And meanwhile, you make a pliant blob of putty out of our bandeirante."

She silenced an angry outburst, whirled away. And she thought: *Our bodies betray us. The Chen-Lhus of the world come along, push buttons, bend us and twist us . . . I won't do it! I won't! This Joao is too nice a guy. But why does he carry that weapon in his pocket?*

I could kill her now and push Johnny off the float, Chen-Lhu thought. *But this is a difficult craft to manage . . . and I'm not experienced in such matters.*

Rhin turned a molten look on him.

Perhaps she'll come around, Chen-Lhu thought. *I know her weaknesses, certainly—but I must be sure.*

Joao returned, slipped into his seat. He brought a fresh smell of wetness into the cabin, but the odor of mildew remained and it was growing stronger.

As the morning wore on, the rain slackened. A warm, misty feeling permeated the cabin's air. Clouds of gunmetal cotton lifted to brush the hilltops above the river and a beaded drapery of raindrops hung on every visible tree.

The pod bobbed and twisted along a swift mud-brown flow accompanied by more and more flotsam—trees, brush, root islands as large as the pod, whole floes of grass and reeds.

Joao drowsed, wondering at the change in Rhin. In their world of the casual liaison, he knew he should merely shrug and make some witty remark. But he didn't feel casual or witty about Rhin. She had touched some chord in him that the pleasures of flesh had never before reached.

Love? he wondered.

But their world had fallen out of the notion of romantic love. There was only family and honor where those things counted and all else involved doing-the-right-thing, which usually meant salvaging the least messy aspects from any situation that happened to fall apart.

No clear way of approaching his problem presented itself. Joao knew only that he was being nudged and pushed from within, that physical weakness contributed to the fuzziness of his thinking . . . and besides, their whole situation was hopeless.

I'm sick, he thought. *The whole world's sick.*

In more ways than one.

A buzzing sound invaded Joao's torpor. He snapped upright, wide awake.

"What's wrong?" Rhin asked.

"Be quiet." He held up a hand to silence her, cocked his head to one side.

Chen-Lhu leaned forward over the back of Joao's seat. "A truck?"

"Yes, by God!" Joao said. "And it's low." He glanced at the sky around them, started to release the canopy, was restrained by Chen-Lhu, who put a hand on his arm.

"Johnny, look there," Chen-Lhu said. He pointed to the left.

Joao turned.

From the shore came what appeared at first to be an odd cloud—wide, thick, moving with a purposeful directness. The cloud resolved itself into a mob of fluttering white, gray and gold insects. They came in at about fifty meters above the pod and the water darkened with their shadow.

The shadow reached out all around the pod and paced it, a moving cover to hide them, from anything in the sky.

As the import of the maneuver penetrated Joao's awareness, he turned, stared at Chen-Lhu. The man's face appeared gray with shock.

"That's . . . deliberate," Rhin whispered.

"How can it be?" Chen-Lhu asked. "How can it be? How can it be?"

In the same moment, Chen-Lhu saw how Joao studied him, realized his own emotions. Anger at himself filled Chen-Lhu. *I must not show fear to these savages!* he thought. He forced himself to sit back, to smile and shake his head.

"To train insects," Chen-Lhu said. "It is almost unbelievable . . . but someone obviously has done it. We see the evidence."

"Please, God," Rhin whispered. "Please."

"Oh, stop your silly prattle, woman," Chen-Lhu said. And even as he spoke, he knew that was the wrong tack to take with Rhin, and he said, "You must remain calm, Rhin. Hysterics serve no purpose."

The rocket sound grew louder.

"Are you sure it's a truck?" Rhin asked. "Perhaps . . ."

"Bandeirante truck," Joao said. "They've rigged it to fire alternate pairs and save fuel. Hear that? That's a bandeirante trick."

"Could they be searching for us?"

"Who knows? Anyway, they're above the clouds."

"And above our friends, too," Chen-Lhu said.

The pulsating counterpoint of rocket motors echoed along the hills. Joao turned his head to follow the sound. It grew fainter upstream, blended with the lapping-swishing-tumbling of the river.

"Won't they come down and look for us?" Rhin pleaded.

"They weren't looking for anyone," Joao said. "They were just going from someplace to someplace."

Rhin looked up at the covering blanket of insects. From this angle and distance, the individuals blended one into another and the whole cloud of them appeared to be one organism.

"We could shoot them down!" she said. She reached for a sprayrifle, but Joao grabbed her arm, stopped her.

"There're still the clouds," he said.

"And our friends have more reinforcements than we have spray charges," Chen-Lhu said. "That I'll wager."

"But if the clouds weren't there," she said. "Won't the clouds ever . . . go away?"

"They may burn off this afternoon," Joao said, and he tried to speak soothingly. "This time of year they do that quite often."

"They're going!" Rhin said. She pointed at the insect cover. "Look! They're going."

Joao looked up to see the fluttering mass start to move back toward the left shore. The shadow accompanied them until they went into the trees and were lost from sight.

"They're gone," Rhin said.

"That only means the truck is no longer with us," Joao said.

Rhin buried her face in her hands, fought down shuddering sobs.

Joao started to caress her neck, to comfort her, but she shook off his hand.

And Chen-Lhu thought: *You must attract him, Rhin, not repel him.*

"We must remember why we are here," Chen-Lhu said. "We must remember what it is we must do."

Rhin sat up, lowering her hands, took a deep breath that hurt the muscles of her chest.

"We must keep ourselves occupied," Chen-Lhu said. "With trivia if necessary. It is a way to prevent . . . fear, boredom, angers. I tell you—I will describe for you an orgy I once attended in Cambodia. There were eight of us, not counting the women—a former prince, the minister of culture . . ."

"We don't want to hear about your damned orgy!" Rhin snapped.

The flesh, Chen-Lhu thought. *She dares not listen to anything that reminds her of her own flesh. That is her weakness, for sure. It is good that I know this.*

"So?" Chen-Lhu said. "Very well. Tell us then about the fine life in Dublin, my dear Rhin. I love to hear of the people who trade wives and mistresses and ride horses and pretend the past has never died."

"You're really a terrible man," Rhin said.

"Excellent!" Chen-Lhu said. "You may hate me, Rhin; I permit it. Hate keeps one occupied, too. One may indulge hate while one thinks about such things as wealth and pleasures. There are times when hate is a much more profitable occupation than making love."

Joao turned, studied Chen-Lhu, hearing the words, seeing he harsh control on the man's face. *He uses words as weapons,* Joao thought. *He maneuvers people and pushes them with words. Doesn't Rhin see this? But of course she doesn't . . . because he's using her for something, wielding her.* For a moment, Joao sat stupefied with discovery.

"You watch me, Johnny," Chen-Lhu said. "What do you think you see?"

Two can play that game, Joao thought. And he said, "I watch a man at work."

Chen-Lhu stared. It wasn't the kind of answer he'd expected—too subtly penetrating and leaving too much uncommitted. He reminded himself that it was difficult to control uncommitted people. Once a man had invested his energies, he could be twisted and turned at will . . . but if the man held back, conserved those energies . . .

"Do you think you understand me, Johnny?" Chen-Lhu asked.

"No, I don't understand you."

"Really, I'm quite uncomplicated; it's not difficult to understand me," Chen-Lhu said.

"That's one of the most complicated statements any man ever made," Joao said.

"Do you mock me?" Chen-Lhu asked, and he put down an upsurge of dismay and anger. Johnny was acting most out of character.

"How could I mock if I don't understand?" Joao asked.

"Something has come over you," Chen-Lhu said. "What is it? You are behaving most strangely."

"Now we understand each other," Joao said.

He goads me, Chen-Lhu thought. *HE goads ME!* And

he asked himself: *Will I have to kill this fool?*

"See how easy it is to keep busy and forget our troubles," Joao said.

Rhin glanced back at Chen-Lhu, saw a smile spread across his face. *He was speaking mostly for my benefit,* she thought. *Wealth and pleasures—that's the price. But what do I pay?* She looked at Joao. *Yes, I hand him a bandeirante on a platter. I give him Joao to use as he sees fit.*

The pod floated backward down the river now, and Rhin stared upstream at hills that disappeared into drifting clouds. *Why do I bother with such questions?* she wondered. *We don't stand a chance. There are only these moments and the opportunity to take whatever pleasure we can from them.*

"Are we down a little on the right side?" Joao asked.

"Perhaps a little," Chen-Lhu said. "Do you think your patch is leaking?"

"It could be."

"Do you have a pump in this stuff?"

"We could use a sprayhead from one of the hand units," Joao said.

Rhin's mind focused now on the weapon in Joao's pocket, and she said, "Joao, don't let them capture me alive."

"Ahh, melodrama," Chen-Lhu said.

"Leave her alone!" Joao snapped. He patted Rhin's hand, looked out and around the pod on all sides. "Why do they leave us alone like this?"

"They've found a new place to wait," Rhin said.

"Always look on the black side," Chen-Lhu said. "What is the worst that could happen, eh? Perhaps they want our heads in the fashion of the aborigines who lived here once."

"You're a great help," Joao said. "Hand me the spray-head off one of those hand units."

"At once, Jefe," Chen-Lhu said, his voice mocking.

Joao accepted the metal and plastic hand pump unit, slipped back to the rear hatch and down to the float. He paused there a moment to study their surroundings.

Not a sign of the creatures he knew were watching them.

Downstream at a bend in the river, a rock escarpment loomed high over the trees—distance perhaps five or six kilometers.

Lava rock, Joao thought. *And the river may have to get through that rock some way.*

He bent to the float, unlocked the inspection plate and probed with the pump. A hollow sloshing echoed from the interior of the pontoon. He braced the pump against the side of the inspection hole, worked the toggle handle. A thin stream of water arched into the river, smelling of poisons from the sprayhead.

The yelping cry of a toucan sounded from the jungle on his right and he could hear the murmur of Chen-Lhu's voice from the cabin.

What is it he talks about when I'm not there? Joao wondered.

He looked up in time to see that the bend in the river was wider than he'd expected. The current carried the pod now away from the rock escarpment. The fact gave Joao no elation. *The river could meander a hundred kilometers through here in this season and return to within a kilometer of where we are now,* he thought.

Rhin's voice lifted suddenly, her words distinct in the damp air: "You son of a bitch!"

And Chen-Lhu answered, "Ancestry is no longer important in my land, Rhin."

The pump sucked air with a wet gurgling, the sound

drowning Rhin's reply. Joao replaced the cap on the inspection hole, returned to the cabin.

Rhin sat with arms folded, face forward. A red blush of anger colored her neck.

Joao wedged the pump into the corner beside the hatch, looked at Chen-Lhu.

"There was water in the float," Chen-Lhu said, his voice smooth. "I heard it."

Yes, I'll bet you did, Joao thought. *What's your game, Dr. Travis Huntington Chen-Lhu? Is it idle sport? Do you goad people for your own amusement, or is it something deeper?*

Joao slipped into his seat.

The pod danced across a pattern of eddy ripples, turned and faced downstream toward a shaft of sunlight that stabbed through the clouds. Slowly, great patches of blue opened in the clouds.

"There's the sun, the good old sun," Rhin said, "now that we don't need it."

A need for male protection came over Rhin, and she leaned her head against Joao's shoulder. "It's going to be sticky hot," she whispered.

"If you'd like to be alone, I could step out on the float," Chen-Lhu mocked.

"Ignore the bastard," Rhin said.

Do I dare ignore him? Joao wondered. *Is that her purpose—to make me ignore him? Do I dare?*

Her hair gave off a scent of musk that threatened to clog Joao's reason. He took a deep breath, shook his head. *What is it with this woman . . . this changeable, mercuric . . . female?*

"You've had lots of girls, haven't you?" Rhin asked.

Her words elicited memory images that flashed through Joao's mind—doe-brown eyes with a distant look of cunning: eyes, eyes, eyes . . . all alike. And lush figures in tight bodices or mounding white sheets . . . warm beneath his hands.

"Any special girl?" Rhin asked.

And Chen-Lhu wondered: *Why does she do this? Is she seeking self justification, reasons to treat him as I wish her to treat him?*

"I've been very busy," Joao said.

"I'll bet you have," she said.

"What's that mean?"

"There's some girl back there in the Green . . . ripe as a mango. What's she like?"

He shrugged, moving her head, but she remained pressed close to him, looking up at his jawline where no beard grew. *He has Indian blood,* she thought. *No beard: Indian blood.*

"Is she beautiful?" Rhin persisted.

"Many women are beautiful," he said.

"One of those dark, full-breasted types, I'll bet," she said. "Have you had her to bed?"

And Joao thought: *What does this mean? That we're all Bohemian types together?*

"A gentleman," Rhin said. "He refused to answer."

She pushed herself up, sat back in her own corner, angry and wondering why she had done that. *Do I torture myself? Do I want this Joao Martinho for my own, to have and to hold? To hell with it!*

"Many families are strict with their women down here," Chen-Lhu said. "Very Victorian."

"Weren't you ever human, Travis?" Rhin asked. "Even for just a day or so?"

"Shut up!" Chen-Lhu barked, and he sat back astonished at himself. *The bitch! How did she get through to me like that?*

Ahhh, Joao thought, *she touched a nerve.*

"What made an animal out of you, Travis?" Rhin asked.

He had himself under control, though, and all he said was, "You have a sharp tongue, my dear. Too bad your mind doesn't match it."

"That's not up to your usual standards, Travis," she said, and she smiled at Joao.

But Joao had heard the crying-out in their voices and he remembered Vierho, the Padre, so solemn, saying, *"A person cries out against life because it's lonely, and because life's broken off from whatever created it. But no matter how much you hate life, you love it, too. It's like a caldron boiling with everything you have to have—but very painful to the lips."*

Abruptly Joao reached out, pulled Rhin to him and kissed her, pressing her against him, digging his hands into her back. Her lips responded after only the briefest hesitation—warm, tingling.

Presently he pulled away, pressed her firmly into her seat and leaned back on his own side.

When she could catch her breath, Rhin said, "Now, what was that all about?"

"There's a little animal in all of us," Joao said.

Does he defend me? Chen-Lhu asked himself, sitting bolt upright. *I don't need defense from such as that!*

But Rhin laughed, shattering his anger, and reached out to caress Joao's cheek. "Isn't there just," she said.

And Chen-Lhu thought: *She is only doing her job. How beautifully she works. Such consummate artistry. It would be a shame to have to kill her.*

9

They have such a talent for occupying themselves with inconsequentials, these humans, the Brain thought. *Even in the face of terrible pressures, they argue and make love and throw trivialities into the air.*

Messengers relays came and went through the rain and sunshine that alternated outside the cave mouth. There was little hesitation over commands now; the essential decision had been made: "Capture or kill the three humans at the chasm; save their heads *in vivo* if you can."

Still, the reports came because the Brain had ordered: "Report to me everything they say."

So much talk of God, the Brain thought. *Is it possible such a Being exists?*

And the Brain reflected that certainly the humans' accomplishments carried an air of grandeur that belied the triviality of their reported actions.

Is it possible this triviality is a code of some sort? the Brain wondered. *But how could it be . . . unless there's more to these emotional inconsequentials and this talk of a God than appears on the surface?*

The Brain had begun its career in logics as a pragmatic atheist. Now doubts began to creep into its computations, and it classified doubt as an emotion.

Still, they must be stopped, the Brain thought. *No matter the cost, they must be stopped. The issue is too important . . . even for this fascinating trio. If they are lost, I shall try to mourn them.*

Rhin felt that they floated in a bowl of burning sunlight with the crippled pod at its center. The cabin was a moist hell pressing in upon her. The drip-drip feeling of perspiration and the smell of bodily closeness, the omnipresent tang of mildew, all of it gnawed at her awareness. Not an animal stirred or cried from either passing shore.

Only an occasional insect flitting across their path reminded her of the watchers in the jungle shadows.

If it wasn't for the bugs, she thought. *The goddamn bugs! And the heat—the goddamn heat.*

An abrupt hysteria seized her and she cried out, "Can't we do anything?"

She began to laugh crazily.

Joao grabbed her shoulders, shook her until she subsided into dry sobs.

"Oh, please, please do something," she begged.

Joao forced all pity out of his voice in the effort to calm her. "Get hold of yourself, Rhin."

"Those goddamn bugs," she said.

Chen-Lhu's voice rumbled at her from the rear of the cabin: "You will please keep in mind, *Doctor Kelly,* that you're an entomologist."

"And I'm going bugs," she said. This struck her as amusing and again she started to laugh. One shake from Joao's arms stopped her. She reached up, took his hands, said, "I'm all right; really I am. It's the heat."

Joao looked into her eyes. "Are you sure?"

"Yes."

She disengaged herself, sat back in her corner, stared out the window. The sweeping passage of shoreline caught her eyes hypnotically: fused movement. It was like time—the immediate past never quite discarded, no fixed starting point for the future—all one, all melted into one gliding, stretched-out forever. . . .

What ever made me choose this career? she wondered.

As though in answer, she found projected upon her memory the full sequence of an event she'd left buried in her childhood. She'd been six and it was the year her father spent in the American West doing his book about Johannes Kelpius. They'd lived in an old adobe house and flying ants had made a nest against the wall. Her father had sent a handyman to burn out the nest and she had crouched to watch. There'd been the smell of kerosene, a sudden burst of yellow flame in sunlight, black smoke and a cloud of whirling insects with pale amber wings enveloping her in their frenzy.

She'd run screaming into the house, winged creatures crawling over her, clinging to her. And in the house: adult anger, hands thrusting her into a bathroom, a voice commanding, "Clean those bugs off you! The very idea, bringing them into the house. See you don't leave a one on the floor. Kill them and flush them down the toilet."

For a time that had seemed forever, she'd screamed and pounded and kicked against the locked door. *"They won't die! They won't die!"*

Rhin shook her head to drive out the memory. "They won't die," she whispered.

"What?" Joao asked.

"Nothing," she said. "What time is it?"

"It'll be dark soon."

She kept her attention on the passing shore—tree ferns and cabbage palms here, with rising water beginning to pour off around their trunks. But the river was wide and its central current still swift. In the spotted sunlight beyond the trees she thought she saw flitting movements of color.

Birds, she hoped.

Whatever they were, the things moved so fast she felt she saw them only after they were gone.

Thick billowings of clouds began filling the eastern horizon with a look of depth and weight and blackness. Lightning flickered soundlessly beneath them. A long interval afterward, the thunder came, a low, sodden hammerstroke.

The heaviness of waiting hung over the river and the jungle. Currents crawled around the pod like writhing serpents—a muddy brown velvet oozing motion that harried the floats: push and turn . . . push, twist and turn.

It's the waiting, Rhin thought.

Tears slipped down her cheeks and she wiped them away.

"Is something wrong, my dear?" Chen-Lhu asked.

She wanted to laugh, but knew laughter would drag her back into hysteria. "If you aren't the banal son of a bitch!" she said. "Something wrong!"

"Ahhh, we still have our fighting spirit," Chen-Lhu said.

Luminous gray darkness of a cloud shadow flowed across the pod, flattened all contrast.

Joao watched a line of rain surge across the water whipped toward him by bursts of wind. Again, lightning flickered. The growl of thunder came faster, sharper. The sound set off a band of howler monkeys on the left shore. Their cries echoed across the water.

Darkness built up its hold on the river. Briefly, the clouds parted in the west and presented a sky like a sheet of burnished turquoise that drifted swiftly from yellow into a deep wine as red as a bishop's cloak. The river looked black and oily. Clouds dropped across the sunset and once more a jagged fire-plume of lightning etched itself against the distance.

The rain took up its endless stammering on the canopy, washing the shorelines into dove-gray mist. Night covered the scene.

"Oh, God, I'm scared," Rhin whispered. "Oh, God, I'm scared. Oh, God, I'm scared."

Joao found he had no words to comfort her. Their world and everything it demanded of them had gone beyond words, all transformed into an elemental flowing indistinguishable from the river itself.

A din of frogs came out of the night and they heard water hissing through reeds. Not even the faintest glow of moonlight penetrated the clouded darkness. Frogs and hissing reeds faded. The pod and its three occupants returned to a world of beating rain suspended above a faint wash of river against floats.

"It's very strange, this being hunted," Chen-Lhu whispered.

The words fell on Joao as though they came from some disembodied source. He tried to recall Chen-Lhu's appearance and was astonished when no image came into his mind. He searched for something to say and all he could find was: "We're not dead yet."

Thank you, Johnny, Chen Lhu thought. *I needed some such nonsense from you to put things into perspective.* He chuckled silently to himself, thinking: *Fear is the penalty of consciousness. There's no weakness in fear . . . only in showing it. Good, evil—it's all a matter of how you view it, with a god or without one.*

"I think we should anchor," Rhin said. "What if we came on rapids in the night before we could hear them? Who could hear anything in this rain?"

"She's right," Chen-Lhu said.

"D'you want to go out there and drop the grapnel, Travis?" Joao asked.

Chen-Lhu felt his mouth go dry.

"Go ahead if you want," Joao said.

No weakness in fear, only in showing it, Chen-Lhu thought. He pictured what might be out there waiting in the darkness—perhaps one of the creatures they'd seen on the shore. Each second's delay, Chen-Lhu realized, betrayed him.

"I think," Joao said, "that it's more dangerous to open the hatch at night than it is to drift . . . and listen."

"We do have the winglights," Chen-Lhu said. "That is, if we hear something." Even as he spoke, he sensed how weak and empty his words were.

Chen-Lhu felt fluid heat ripple through his veins, anger like a series of velvet explosions. Still, the unknown remained out there, a place of ravenous tranquility, full of furiously remembered brilliance even in this blackness.

Fear strips away all pretense, Chen-Lhu thought. *I've been dishonest with myself.*

It was as though the thought thrust him suddenly around a corner, there to confront himself like a reflection in a mirror. And he was both substance and reflection. The abruptly awakening clarity sent memories streaking through his mind until he felt his entire past dancing and weaving like fabric rolling off a loom—reality and illusion in the same cloth.

The sensation passed, leaving him feverish with an inner trembling and a sense of terrible loss.

I'm having a delayed reaction to the insect poisons, he thought.

"Oscar Wilde was a pretentious ass," Rhin said. "Any number of lives are worth any number of deaths. Bravery has nothing to do with that."

Even Rhin defends me, Chen-Lhu thought.

The thought enraged him.

'You God-fearing fools," he snarled. "All of you chanting: 'Thou hast *being*, God!' There couldn't be a god without man! A god wouldn't know he existed if it weren't for man! If there ever was a god . . . this universe is his mistake!"

Chen-Lhu fell silent, surprised to find himself panting as though after great exertion.

A burst of rain hammered against the canopy as though in some celestial answer, then faded into wet muttering.

"Well . . . would you listen to the atheist," Rhin said.

Joao peered into the darkness where her voice had originated, suddenly angry with her, feeling shame in her words. Chen-Lhu's outburst had been like seeing the man naked and defenseless. The thing should've been ignored, not given substance by comment. Joao felt that Rhin's words had served only to drive Chen-Lhu into a corner.

The thought made him recall a scene out of his days in North America, a vacation with a classmate in eastern Oregon. He'd been hunting quail along a fenceline when two of his host's mismatched brindle hounds had burst over a rise in pursuit of a scrawny bitch coyote. The coyote had seen the hunter and had swerved left only to be trapped in a fence corner.

In that corner, the coyote, a symbol of cowardice, had whirled and slashed the two dogs into bloody cravens that had fled with tails between legs. Joao, awed, had watched and allowed the coyote to escape.

Remembering that scene, Joao sensed that it encapsulated the problem of Chen-Lhu. *Something or someone has trapped that man in a corner.*

"I am going to sleep now," Chen-Lhu said. "Awaken me at midnight. And please—do not become so distracted that you fail to peer ahead with your ears."

To hell with you! Rhin thought. And she made no attempt at silence as she pushed herself across the seat into Joao's arms.

"We must place part of our force below the rapids," the Brain commanded, "in case the humans escape the net as they did before. They must not escape this time." And the Brain added here the overhive-survival-fear-threat symbol to produce the greatest degree of angry alertness among messengers and action groups.

"Give the *little-deadlies* careful instructions," the Brain ordered. "If the vehicle eludes our net and passes the rapids *safely*, all three humans must be killed."

Golden winged messengers danced their confirmation on the ceiling, fluttered out of the cave into the gray light that soon would be night.

These three humans have been interesting, even informative, the Brain thought, *but now it must end. We have other humans, after all . . . and emotion must not figure in the logical necessities.*

But these thoughts only aroused more of the Brain's newly learned emotions and brought the nurse insects scurrying to adjust their charge's unusual demands.

Presently the Brain put aside the subject of the three humans on the river and began to worry about the fate of its simulacra somewhere beyond the barriers.

Human radio carried no reports that the simulacra had been discovered . . . but this meant nothing really. Such reports might be suppressed. Unless they could be located by their own kind and warned (and that soon), the simulacra would come out. The danger was great and the time short.

The Brain's agitation brought its attendants to a step they seldom took. Narcotics were brought up and administered. The Brain sank into a lethargic, drowsing half-sleep where its dreams transformed it into a creature like the humans, and it stalked a dream trail with a rifle in its hands.

Even in its dream, the Brain worried lest the *game* elude it. And here the nurse insects could not reach and minister. The worry continued.

Joao awoke at dawn to find the river cloaked by a restless drapery of fog. He felt stiff and cramped, his thoughts confused by a feverish sensation as fuzzy as the fog on the river. The sky held the color of platinum.

An island shrouded by the fog's ghost-smoke loomed ahead. The current moved the pod to the right past matchstick piles of logs and flooded remnants of bushes and grass that bent downstream and vibrated with the current.

The pod floated definitely low on the right. Joao knew he should go out and pump the float. He knew he had the energy to do the job, but he couldn't find energy to set himself into motion.

Rhin's voice intruded: "When did the rain stop?"

Chen-Lhu answered from the rear, "Just before dawn." He began to cough, then: "Still no sign of our friends."

"We're floating low on the right," Rhin said.

"I was about to see to that," Chen-Lhu said. "Johnny, I presume I just put the sprayhead tube into the float and work the toggle?"

Joao swallowed, astonished at how grateful he felt that Chen-Lhu had volunteered for this job.

"Johnny?"

"Yes ... that's all you do," Joao said. "The inspection hole in the float has a simple snaplock."

Joao lay back, closed his eyes. He heard Chen-Lhu go out the hatch.

Rhin looked at Joao, noting how tired he appeared. His closed eyes were death's-head sockets rimmed with shadow.

My latest lover, she thought *Death.*

The thought confused her and she wondered at herself that she could find no warmth of feeling this morning toward the man who had drugged her with passion during the night. *A tristia post coitum* had seized her, and now Joao seemed merely another mote of awareness that had touched her quite by accident and paused to share a moment of explosive brilliance.

There was no love in that thought.

Nor hate.

Her feelings now were as nearly sexless and clinical as they'd ever been. The coupling in the night had been a mutual experience, but morning had reduced it to something without savor.

She turned away, looked downstream.

The fog mist had thinned. Through it she glimpsed a black face of lava rock perhaps two kilometers distant. It was difficult to judge the distance, but it towered above the jungle like a ghost ship.

She heard air sucking in the pump then and noted how the pod had returned to an almost level position.

Presently, Chen-Lhu returned. He brought a brief air of cold dampness that stopped when he sealed the hatch.

"It's almost cold out there," he said. "What's the altimeter reading, Johnny?"

Joao aroused himself, peered at the dash. "Six hundred and eight meters."

"How far do you think we've come?"

Joao shrugged, remained silent.

"As much as a hundred and fifty kilometers?" Chen-Lhu asked.

Joao looked out at the flooded banks rushing past, at the current sucking gnarled, obscene roots. "Perhaps."

Perhaps, Chen-Lhu thought. And he wondered why he felt so exhilarated and full of energy. He was actually hungry! He dug for the ration packets, distributed them, then ate in wolfing gulps.

A barrage of rain whipped against the windshield. The pod turned and dipped. Another blast of wind shook them. The pod skittered in it across lines of slapping wavelets. The wind diminished, but the rain continued in sheets that blotted all color from the passing shores. The wind died entirely, but still the rain fell, its drops so thick they appeared to jiggle and dance horizontally.

Joao stared out at a mottled granite shore that passed like a surrealist backdrop. The river appeared at least a kilometer wide here, its dirty brown surface turgid and rolling and spotted by clumps of trees, floating sedge islands, drifting logs.

Abruptly, the pod lurched. Something bumped and scraped beneath the floats. Joao held his breath in fear the patched float would be opened to the torrent.

"Shallows?" Chen-Lhu asked.

A water-logged snag lifted out of the river on their left, rolled and dived like a live thing.

Rhin whispered, "The float. . . ."

"It seems to be holding," Joao said.

A green beetle darted in over the snag, landed on the windshield, waved its antennae at them and departed.

"Anything that happens to us, they're interested," Chen-Lhu said.

Rhin said, "That snag—you don't think . . ."

"I'm ready to believe anything," Chen-Lhu said.

Rhin closed her eyes, muttered, "I hate them! I hate them!"

The rain slackened, fell off to occasional drops that spattered the river or thudded against the canopy. Rhin opened her eyes to see pale avenues of blue opening and closing in the clouds.

"Is it clearing?" she asked.

"What's the difference?" Chen-Lhu asked.

Joao stared out across the rain-flattened grass of a savannah that appeared on their left. The grass ended at an oily green jungle wall some two hundred meters back.

As he looked, a figure emerged from the jungle and waved and beckoned until they drifted out of sight.

"What was that?" Rhin asked, and there was hysteria in her voice.

The distance was too great for certainty, but the figure had looked to Joao like the Padre.

"Vierho?" he whispered.

"It had his appearance, I thought," Chen-Lhu said. "You don't suppose . . ."

"I suppose nothing!"

Ahh, Chen-Lhu thought. *The bandeirante is beginning to break down.*

"I hear something," Rhin said. "It sounds like rapids."

Joao straightened, listened. A faint roaring came to him. "Probably just wind in the trees," he said. But even as he spoke he knew it was not the wind.

"It is rapids," Chen-Lhu said. "See that cliff ahead?"

They stared downstream until gusts of wind pushed a black line up the river toward them and pulled a rain veil over the cliff. The downpour whipped around the pod, thudded onto the canopy. As quickly as it had come, the wind passed, and the current slid them forward through a hiss of rain. Presently even the rain faded, and the river with its slick appearance of secret turbulence stretched out like a tabletop display composed on a mirror.

The pod became for Chen-Lhu a toy miniature shrunken by witchery and lost in an immensity of flood.

Over it all stood the black face of the cliff, growing more and more solid with each second.

Chen-Lhu moved his head slowly from side to side, wondering how he knew what they must face beneath that cliff. He felt that he drifted in a moist pocket of air that drained his life from him. The air carried a smell of physical substance, the dank piling of life and death on the forest floor around the river. Rotting and festering odors came over him. Each carried its message: *"They are there ahead . . . waiting."*

"The pod . . . it won't fly now, will it?" Chen-Lhu asked.

"I don't think I can get that float off the river," Joao said. He wiped perspiration from his forehead, closed his eyes and experienced the nightmare sensation of dreaming through the entire trip to this point. His eyes snapped open.

Stagnant silence settled over the cabin.

The roar of rapids grew louder, but there was still no view of the white water.

A flock of golden-beaked toucans lifted from a stand of palms at a downstream bend. They climbed in a frenzied cloud, filling the air with their dog-pack yelps. Then they were gone and the sound of the rapids remained. The cliff loomed above the palms just around the bend.

"We have five or six minutes of fuel . . . maybe," Joao said. "I think we should go around that bend under power."

"Agreed," Chen-Lhu said. He fastened his safety harness.

Rhin heard the sound, buckled her own harness.

Joao found the cold buckles of his harness beside him, snapped them in place as he studied the dash. His hands began to tremble as he thought of the delicacy required in manipulating the throttle. *I've done it twice*, he told himself.

But there was no comfort in that. He knew he was at the edge of his energy . . . and his reason.

A curving ripple of current fanned away from the left shore where the river turned downstream. The water there began to glisten and sparkle. Joao looked up to see cracks of blue striking through the clouds. He took a deep breath, pressed the igniter, counted.

The warning light blinked out.

Joao eased the throttle ahead. The motors banged, then mounted to a steady roar. The pod began to pick up speed, danced through the ripple track. She was right-side heavy and a dull sloshing could be heard from the float there.

It'll never lift, Joao thought. He felt feverish and only loosely connected to his senses.

The pod made its racketing, sluggish way around the bend . . . and there it stood, the lava wall, no more than a kilometer downstream. The river ran through the wall in a notch that rose like something split out by a giant axe. Sheer black heights of rock compressed the water at their base into a tumbling agony.

"Jeeeesus," Joao whispered.

Rhin clutched his arm. "Turn back! You've got to turn back."

"We can't," Joao said. "There's no other way."

Still, his hand hesitated on the throttle. Press forward on that knob and risk explosion? There was no alternative. He could see waves in the chasm now cresting over unseen rocks, shooting milk-and-amber mist upward.

With a convulsive movement, Joao slammed the throttle ahead. The roar of the rockets drowned out the water's sound.

Joao prayed to the float: "Hold together . . . please . . . hold together."

Abruptly, the pod lifted onto its steps, began skimming faster and faster. In that instant, Joao saw movement on both shores beside the chasm. Something lifted dripping and snakelike across the entrance to the gorge.

"Another net!" Rhin screamed.

Joao saw the net with a dreamlike detachment, knew he couldn't avoid it. The pod skidded over a cross-eddy and onto a glossy black pool inhabited by that dripping barrier. He saw the dark pattern of net squares and, through them, water creased into steeper and steeper furrows that flashed outward and down into the chasm.

The pod slammed into the net, pulled it, stretching it, tearing it. Joao was thrown forward against his harness as the pod tipped down by the nose. He felt the back of the seat slam his ribs. There came a thunderous tearing-grinding-bubbling sound and a sudden giving away.

The motors stopped short—flooded out or unable to suck fuel. The roaring of the water filled the cabin.

Joao pulled himself up by the wheel, looked around. The pod floated almost level, turning. But his eyes interpreted the motion as the world turning around him— black wall, green line of jungle, white water.

The pod slid down a sloping current to the right,

crunched against the first obsidian buttress above the
torrent. A scraping, wrenching of metal competed with
the chasm's roar.

Rhin screamed something that was lost in the ava-
lanche sound of water.

The pod bounced outward from the rock wall,
whirled, pounded across two infolding steps of explosive current. Metal creaked and groaned. The spiral
cone of a whirlpool sucked at the floats, shot them sideways into a lifting tipping, pounding delirium of motion.

A vast pulsing-rumbling like ocean waves on rocks
deafened Joao. He saw a glistening ledge of black rock,
its face carved by the current, loom directly ahead. The
pod smashed into it, recoiled. And Joao found himself
torn from his harness, on the floor, tangled with Rhin.
He grabbed the base of the wheel with his right hand.

Above him the canopy buckled. He watched in un-
believing shock as the canopy tipped forward and disappeared. He saw the left wing crumple upward against
rock. The pod whipped around to the right, presenting
a blurred arc of sky and another black wall.

A crazy rumbling from the shattered wing added to
the din.

Joao thought: *We aren't going to make it. Nothing
can survive this.*

He felt Rhin with both arms around his waist clinging
in terror, her voice in his left ear: "Please make it stop;
please make it stop."

Joao saw the pod's nose lift, slam down, saw white
water and spume boil past where the canopy had been.
He saw a sprayrifle jerk out that opening into the river,
and he wedged himself more tightly between the seats
and the dash. His fingers ached where he clutched the
wheel. A wrenching motion of the pod turned his head

and he saw Chen-Lhu's arms wrapped around the seat back directly above him.

Chen-Lhu felt the sound like a direct contact on his nerves magnified almost beyond endurance. It grated through him in an unchecked rhythm, dominated his world: a deafening cymbal dissonance gone wild in counterpoint, a rasping, crunching, maelstrom grating. He felt that he had become a seeing-hearing-feeling receptor without any other function.

Rhin pressed her face against Joao. Everything was the hot smell of Joao's body and insane motion. She felt the pod lift . . . lift . . . lift and slam down, twisting, turning. Up. Down. Up. Down. Up. Down. It was like some crazy kind of sex. A staccato punching motion shook her as the pod shot down a washboard of rapids.

Joao felt all his consciousness concentrated into the terrible intensity of sight. He saw directly out an opening in the cabin side where no opening should be—a millrace chute, a black cavity of water, solid spray, damp green shade along a scarred cliff. He looked directly down into a frothed spiral of current as the pod tipped. His hand was numb where he clutched the wheel. His shoulder ached.

A brown turtleback of current rolled over directly in front of the opening. Joao felt the pod slide up onto that smoothness with a deceptively gentle gliding motion, saw the river drop away beyond.

She can't take any more, he told himself.

The pod nosed down, faster and faster. Joao braced himself against the dash. He saw a green-brown wave curl upward past a shattered wing stump—up . . . up . . . up . . .

The pod smashed through it.

Green darkness and water cascaded into the cabin. There came a screech of metal. Joao felt the tail slam down, lifting him into washed twilight. He clawed his way toward the seat, dragging Rhin with him, saw Chen-Lhu's arms still wrapped there, water pouring from the torn side of the cabin. He felt the tail section rip across rocks as the pod shot across another boiling mound of water.

Glaring sunlight!

Joao twisted around, half blinded by the brilliance. He stared past a torn hole where the motors had been, looked back up the gorge. The roaring noise of the place blasted at him. He saw the insane waves, the violence, and he thought: *Did we really come through that?*

He felt water around his ankles, turned, expecting to see another crazy descent of rapids. But there was only a broad pool—dark water all around. It absorbed the turbulence of the gorge and for all that violence showed only glistening bubbles and the swift spreading and converging of current runnels.

The pod lurched under him. Joao staggered in the water, clutched the right lip of the cabin, looked down at the remaining wing which appeared to float just on the surface of the river.

Rhin's voice broke across the moment with a shocking tone of normality: "Hadn't we better get out? We're sinking."

Joao tried to shake off his feeling of detachment, looked down to see her seated in her seat. He heard Chen-Lhu struggle upright behind her, coughing, saw the man loom there.

There came a metallic gurgling and the right wing dipped beneath the surface.

It occurred to Joao then with a twisted sense of elation that they were still alive . . . but the pod was dead. Elation drained from him.

"We gave them a good run for their money," Chen-

Lhu said, "but I think this is the end of the line."

"Is it?" Joao growled. He felt anger boil in him, touched the bulge of Vierho's big blunderbuss pistol in his pocket. The reflex motion, the foolish emptiness of it, brought a wave of crazy amusement into his mind.

Imagine trying to kill those things with this gun, he thought.

"Joao?" Rhin said.

"Yes." He nodded to her, turned, climbed out onto the edge of the cabin, straightened, balancing there to study their surroundings. A damp spray mist from the gorge blew across him.

"This thing's not going to stay afloat much longer," Chen-Lhu said. He looked back up the chasm, his mind suddenly refusing to accept what had happened to them.

"I could swim to that point down there," Rhin said. "How about the rest of you?"

Chen-Lhu turned, saw a treeless finger of land jutting into their pool about a hundred meters downstream. It was a fragile tentacle of reeds and dirt poised on the water and backed by a high wall of trees. Long dragging marks slanted along the mud below the reeds into the river.

Alligator sign, Chen-Lhu thought.

"I see 'gator sign," Joao said. "Best stick with the pod as long as we can."

Rhin felt terror rise in her throat, whispered, "Will it float much longer?"

"If we hold very still," Joao said. "We seem to've trapped some air under us somewhere—maybe in the wing and that left float."

"No sign of . . . *them* here," Rhin said.

"They'll be along presently," Chen-Lhu said, and he was surprised at the casual tone of his own voice.

Joao studied the little peninsula.

The pod drifted away, then returned in a back eddy until only a few meters separated the partly submerged wing's tip from the muddy shore.

Where're those damned alligators? he wondered.

"We're not going to get any closer," Chen-Lhu said.

Joao nodded agreement, said, "You first, Rhin. Stay on the wing as long as you can. We'll be right with you." He put his hand on the pistol in his pocket, helped her up with the other hand. She slid down to the wing and it tipped farther under until stopped by the mud below the shore.

Chen-Lhu slid down behind her, said, "Let's go!"

They splashed ashore, their feet sinking in mud when they left the wing. Joao smelled rocket fuel, saw its painted whorls on the river. The reed embankment lifted ahead of him with the tracks of Rhin and Chen-Lhu in it. He climbed up beside them, stared toward the jungle.

"Would it be possible to reason with them?" Chen-Lhu asked.

Joao lifted the sprayrifle, said, "I think this is the only argument we have." He looked at the rifle's charge, saw it was full, turned back to study the remains of the pod. It lay almost submerged, its wing anchored in the mud, brown current lapping around and through the torn holes in the cabin.

"You think we should try to get more weapons out of the pod?" Chen-Lhu asked. "To what purpose? We are going nowhere from here."

He's right, of course, Joao thought. He saw that Chen-Lhu's words had set Rhin to shivering uncontrollably, and he put an arm around her until the shivering stopped.

"Such a lovely little domestic scene," Chen-Lhu said, staring at them. And he thought: *They're the only coin*

I have. Perhaps our friends will bargain—two without a fight for one to go free.

Rhin felt calmness return. Joao's arm around her, his silence, had shaken her more than anything she cared to remember. Such a little thing, she thought. *Just a brotherly-fatherly hug.*

Chen-Lhu coughed. She looked at him.

"Johnny," Chen-Lhu said. "Give me the sprayrifle. I'll cover you while you try to get more weapons from the pod."

"You said it yourself," Joao said. "To what purpose?"

Rhin pulled out of Joao's embrace, suddenly terrified by the look in Chen-Lhu's eyes.

"Give me the rifle," Chen-Lhu said, his voice flat.

What's the difference? Joao asked himself. He looked up into Chen-Lhu's eyes, saw the unblinking savagery there. Good God! *What's come over him?* He found himself obsessed by the man's eyes, their glaring impact, the almond frames for rage.

Chen-Lhu's left foot shot out, caught Joao's left arm, sent the rifle pitching skyward. Joao felt his arm go numb, but fell back instinctively into the stance of the *capoeira*, the Brazilian judo. Almost blind with pain, he dodged another kick, leaped to one side.

"Rhin, the rifle!" Chen-Lhu shouted. And he stalked after Joao.

Rhin's mind refused to function for a moment. She shook her head, looked to where the rifle had fallen butt first into the reeds. It pointed skyward, its stock in the mud. *The rifle?* she asked herself. Well, yes, it would stop a man at this range. She retrieved the rifle, brought it up with mud and torn reeds clinging to its stock, aimed it toward the two men dodging and posturing as though in some weird dance.

Chen-Lhu saw her, leaped backward, crouched.

Joao straightened, clutching his injured arm.

"All right, Rhin," Chen-Lhu said. "Pick him off."

With a feeling of horror at herself, Rhin found the muzzle of the rifle swinging toward Joao.

Joao started to reach for the weapon in his pocket, stopped. He felt only a sick emptiness coupled with despair. *Let her kill me if she's going to*, he thought.

Rhin gritted her teeth, brought the rifle back to bear on Chen-Lhu.

"Rhin!" he said, and started toward her.

You son of a bitch! she thought, and squeezed the trigger.

A hard stream of poison and butyl carrier leaped from the muzzle, slammed into Chen-Lhu, staggered him. He tried to fight his way through it, but the stream caught him in the face, knocked him down. He rolled and writhed, fighting an increasing entanglement as the carrier coagulated. His movements became slower—jerking, stopping, jerking.

Rhin stood with the rifle pointed at Chen-Lhu until its charge ran dry, then hurled the weapon from her.

Chen-Lhu gave one last jerking, convulsive movement, lay still. No feature of the man remained exposed; he was merely a sticky gray-black-orange mass in the reeds.

Rhin found she was panting, swallowed, tried to take a deep breath, but couldn't.

Joao crossed to her side and she saw that he had the pistol in his hand. His left hand dangled uselessly at his side.

"Your arm," she said.

"Broken," he said. "Look at the trees."

She turned as directed, saw flitting movements in the shadows. A puff of wind troubled the leaves there, and an Indian shape appeared in front of the jungle. It was as though he had been flung there by sorcery that produced his image in one movement. Ebony eyes glittered with that faceted sparkle beneath a straight slash of bangs. Red whorls of achiote streaked the face. Scarlet macaw feathers protruded from a string binding the deltoid muscles of the left arm. He wore a breech clout with monkeyskin bag dangling from the waist.

The remarkable accuracy of the simulacrum struck through her terror, then Rhin remembered the flying ants of her childhood and the gray fluttering wave that had engulfed the IEO camp. She turned toward Joao, pleading, "Joao . . . Johnny: please, *please* shoot me. Don't let them take me."

He wanted to turn and run, but muscles refused to obey.

"If you love me," she pleaded. "Please."

He couldn't avoid the pleading in her voice. The gun came up as though of its own volition, point blank.

"I love you, Joao," she whispered, and closed her eyes.

Joao found himself blinded by tears. He saw her face through a mist. *I must,* he thought. *God help me—I must.* Convulsively, he jerked the trigger.

The gun roared, bucking in his hand.

Rhin jerked backward as though pushed by a giant hand. She half turned and pitched face down into the reeds.

Joao whirled away, unable to look, stared down at the pistol in his hand. Movement by the trees attracted him. He shook away the tears, stared at the line of creatures trailing out of the forest. There were the ones like the *sertao* Indians who had kidnaped him with his father . . . more forest Indians . . . the figure of Thome from his own band . . . another man, thin and in a black suit, hair shiny silver.

Even my father! Joao thought. *They copy even my father!*

He brought the pistol up, its muzzle pointing at his heart. He felt no rage, only an enormous sorrow as he pulled the trigger.

Darkness slammed him.

10

There was a dream of being carried, a dream of tears and shouting, a dream of violent protests and defiance and rejection.

Joao awoke to yellow-orange light and the figure that could not be his father bending over him, thrusting a hand out, saying, "Then examine my hand if you don't believe!"

It cannot be my father, Joao thought. *I am dead ... he is dead. They've copied him ... mimicry, nothing more.*

Numbing shock invaded Joao's awareness then.

How am I here? he wondered. His mind searched back through memories and he saw himself killing Rhin with Vierho's old blunderbuss, then turning the weapon on himself.

Something moved behind the figure that couldn't be his father. Joao's attention jerked that way, saw a giant face at least two meters tall. It was a baleful face in the strange light, eyes brilliant and glaring. . . . enormous eyes with pupils within pupils. The face turned and Joao saw that it could be no more than two centimeters thick. Again, the face turned. The strange eyes focused toward Joao's feet.

Joao forced himself to look down, lifting his head, then falling back with a violent trembling. Where his feet should have been he'd seen a foaming green cocoon. Joao lifted his left hand, remembering that it had been broken, but the arm came up without pain and he saw that his skin shared the green tones of that repellent cocoon.

"Examine my hand!" ordered the old-man figure beside him. "I command it!"

"He is not quite awake."

It was a booming voice, resonant, shaking the air all around them, and it seemed to Joao that the voice came from somewhere beneath that giant face.

What nightmare is this? Joao asked himself. *Am I in hell?*

With an abrupt, violent motion, Joao reached up, clutched the proffered hand.

It felt warm . . . human.

Tears flooded Joao's eyes. He shook his head to clear them, remembered . . . somewhere . . . doing that same thing. But there were more pressing matters than memories. The hand felt real . . . his tears felt real.

"How can this be?" he whispered.

"Joao, my son," said his father's voice.

Joao peered up at the familiar face. It was his father and no mistaking, down to the very last feature. "But . . . your heart," Joao said.

"My pump," the old man said. "Look." He pulled his hand away, turned to display where the back of his suit had been cut away. Its edges appeared to be held by some gummy substance. An oily yellow surface pulsed between those fabric edges.

Joao saw the hair-fine scale lines, the multiple shapes. He recoiled.

So it was a copy, another of their tricks.

The old man turned back to face him, and Joao couldn't avoid the youthful look of glee in the eyes. They weren't faceted, those eyes.

"The old pump failed and they gave me a new one," his father said. "It shares my blood and lives off me. It'll give me a few more useful years. What do you think our medical men will say about that?"

"It's really you," Joao gasped.

"All except the pump," the old man said. "But you, you stupid fool! What a mess you made of yourself and that poor woman."

"Rhin," Joao whispered.

"Blew out your hearts and parts of your lungs," his father said. "And you fell right into the middle of all that corrosive poison you'd sprayed all over the landscape. They not only had to give the two of you new hearts, but whole new blood systems!"

Joao lifted his hands, stared at the green skin. He felt dazzled by it and unable to escape a dream quality in his surroundings.

"They know medical tricks we haven't even imagined," his father said. "I haven't been this excited since I was a boy. I can hardly wait to get back and . . . Joao! What is it?"

Joao thrust himself up, glared at the old man. "We're not human anymore! We're not human if . . . We're not human!"

"Oh, be still," his father ordered.

"If this is . . . They're in control!" Joao protested. He forced his gaze onto the giant face behind his father. "They'll *rule* us!"

He sank back, gasping.

"We'll be their slaves," Joao whispered.

"Such foolishness," the drum-voice rumbled.

"He always was melodramatic," the elder Martinho said. "Look at the mess he made of things out there on the river. Of course, *you* had a hand in that. If you'd only listened to me, trusted me."

"Now we have a hostage," the Brain rumbled. "Now we can afford to trust you."

"You've had a hostage ever since you put this pump in me," the old man said.

"I didn't understand the price you put on the individual unit," the Brain said. "After all, *we'll* spend almost any unit to save the hive."

"Not a queen," the old man said. "You won't spend a queen. And how about yourself? Would you spend yourself?"

"Unthinkable," the Brain muttered.

Slowly, Joao turned his head, looked beneath the giant face to where the voice originated. He saw a white mass about four meters across, a pulsing yellow sac protruding from it. Wingless insects crawled over it, into fissures along its surface and along the stone floor of the cave underneath. The face reared up from that mass supported by dozens of round stalks. Their scaled surfaces betrayed their nature.

The reality of the situation began to penetrate Joao's shock.

"Rhin?" he whispered.

"Your mate is safe," the Brain rumbled. "Changed like yourself, but safe."

Joao continued to stare at the white mass on the cave floor. He saw that the voice issued from the pulsing yellow sac.

"Your attention *is* drawn to our way of answering your threat to us," the Brain said. "This is our brain. It is vulnerable, yet strong . . . just as your brain."

Joao fought down a shiver of revulsion.

"Tell me," the Brain said, "how you define slave."

"I'm a slave now," Joao whispered. "I'm in bondage to you. I must obey you or you can kill me."

"But you tried to kill yourself," the Brain said.

The thought unfolded and unfolded in Joao's awareness.

"A slave is one who must produce wealth for another," the Brain said. "There is only one true wealth in all the universe. I have given you some of it. I have given your father and your mate some of it. And your friends. This wealth is living time. Time. Are we slaves because we have given you more time to live?"

Joao looked up from the voice sac to the giant, glittering eyes. He thought he detected amusement there.

"We've spared and extended the lives of all those who were with you," the voice drummed. "That makes us your slaves, does it not?"

"What do you take in return?" Joao demanded.

"Ah, hah!" the voice fairly barked. "Quid pro quo! That's this thing called business which I didn't understand. Your father will leave soon to speak with the men of his government. He is our messenger. He trades us his time. He is our slave as well, is it not so? We are tied to each other by the bond of mutual slavery that cannot be broken. It never could be broken . . . no matter how hard you tried."

"It's very simple once you understand the interdependence," Joao's father said.

"Understand what?"

"Some of our kind lived once in greenhouses," the voice rumbled. "Their cells remembered the experience. You know about greenhouses, of course."

The giant face turned to look out at the cavemouth,

where dawn was beginning to touch the world with gray. "That out there, that, too, is a greenhouse." Again, it peered down at Joao, the giant eyes glittering. "To sustain life, a greenhouse must be maintained in a delicate state of balance by the life within it—enough of this chemical, enough of that one, another substance available when required. That which is poison one day can be the sweetest food the next day."

"What's all this to do with slavery?" Joao demanded, and he heard the petulance in his own voice.

"Life has developed through millions of years on greenhouse Earth," the Brain rumbled. "Sometimes it developed in the poison excrement of other life . . . and then that poison became necessary to it. Without a substance produced by wireworms, that savannah grass out there would die . . . in time."

Joao stared up at the rock ceiling, his thoughts turning over like cards in a file. "China's barren earth!" he said.

"Precisely," the Brain said. "Without substances produced by . . . *insects*, and other forms of life, your kind of life would perish. Sometimes just a faint trace of the substance is needed, such as the special copper produced by arachnids. Sometimes the substance must pass through many valences, subtly changed each time, before it can be used by a life form at the end of the chain. Break the chain and all die. The more different forms of life there are, the more life the greenhouse can support. The successful greenhouse must enclose many forms of life—the more forms of life, the healthier for all."

"Chen-Lhu," Joao said. "He could be made to help. He could go with my father, tell them . . . Did you save Chen-Lhu?"

"The Chinese," the Brain said. "He can be said to

live, although you abused him cruelly. The essential
structures of the brain are alive, thanks to our prompt
action."

Joao looked down at the bulging, fissured mass on
the floor of the cave. He turned away.

"They have given me proof to take back with me,"
Joao's father said. "There can be no doubt. No one will
doubt. We must stop killing and changing insects."

"And let them take over," Joao whispered.

"We say you must stop killing yourselves," the voice
rumbled. "Already the people of your Chen-Lhu are . . .
I believe you would call it *reinfesting* their land. Perhaps they will be in time, perhaps not. Here, it is not
too late. In China, they were efficient and thorough . . .
and they may need our help."

"But you'll be our masters," Joao said. And he
thought: *Rhin . . . Rhin, where are you?*

"We'll merely achieve a new balance," the Brain
said. "It will be interesting to see. But there will be time
to discuss this later. You are quite free to move . . . and
capable of it. Just do not come too close to me: my
nurses will not permit that. But for now, feel free to
join your mate outside. There is sunshine this morning.
Let the sun work on your skin and on the chlorophyll
in your blood. And when you come back here, tell me
if the sun is your slave."

*In the desert, the line between life and death
is sharp and quick.*

—Zensunni fire poetry from Arrakis

Far from thinking machines and the League of Nobles, the desert never changed. The Zensunni descendants who had fled to Arrakis scraped out squalid lives in isolated cave communities, barely subsisting in a harsh environment. They experienced little enjoyment, yet fought fiercely to remain alive for just another day.

Sunlight poured across the ocean of sand, warming dunes that rippled like waves breaking upon an imagined shore. A few black rocks poked out of the dust like islands, but offered no shelter from the heat or the demon worms.

This desolate landscape was the last thing he would ever see. The people had accused him, chosen the young man as a scapegoat, and would mete out their punishment. His innocence was not relevant.

"Begone, Selim!" came a shout from the caves above. "Go far from here!" He recognized the voice of his young friend—*former* friend—Ebrahim. Perhaps the other boy was relieved, since by rights it should have been him facing exile and death, not Selim. But no one would mourn the loss of an orphan, and so Selim had been cast out in the Zensunni version of justice.

A raspy voice said, "May the worms spit out your scrawny hide." That was old Glyffa, who had once been like a mother to him. "Thief! Water stealer!"

From the caves, the tribe began to throw stones. One sharp rock struck the cloth he had wrapped around his dark hair for protection against the sun. Selim ducked, but did not give them the satisfaction of seeing him cringe. They had stripped almost everything from him, but as long as he drew breath they would never take his pride.

Naib Dhartha, the sietch leader, leaned out. "The tribe has spoken. Your fate rests on your own crimes, Selim."

Protestations of his innocence would do no good, nor would excuses or explanations. Keeping his balance on the steep path, the young man stooped to grab a sharp-edged stone. He held it in his palm and glared up at the people.

Selim had always been skilled at throwing rocks. He could pick off ravens, small kangaroo mice, or lizards for the community cookpot. If he aimed carefully, he could have put out one of the Naib's eyes. Selim had seen Dhartha whispering quietly with Ebrahim's father, watched them form their plan to cast the blame on him instead of the guilty boy. They had decided Selim's punishment using measures other than the truth.

Naib Dhartha had dark eyebrows and jet-black hair bound into a ponytail by a dull metal ring. A purplish geometric tattoo of dark angles and straight lines marked his left cheek. His wife had drawn it on his face using a steel needle and the juice of a scraggly inkvine the Zensunni cultivated in their terrarium gardens. The Naib glared down as if daring Selim to throw the stone, because the Zensunni would respond with a pummeling barrage of large rocks.

But such a punishment would kill him far too quickly. Instead, the tribe would drive Selim away from their tight-knit community. And on Arrakis, one did not survive without help. Existence in the desert required cooperation, each person doing his part. The Zensunni looked upon stealing—especially the theft of water—as the worst crime imaginable.

Selim pocketed the stone. Ignoring the jeers and insults, he continued his tedious descent toward the open desert.

Dhartha intoned in a voice that sounded like a bass howl of stormwinds, "Selim, who has no father or mother—Selim, who was welcomed as a member of our tribe—you have been found guilty of stealing tribal water. Therefore, you must walk across the sands." Dhartha raised his voice, shouting before the condemned man could pass out of earshot. "May Shaitan choke on your bones."

All his life, Selim had done more work than most others. Because he was of unknown parentage, the tribe demanded it of him. No one helped him when he was sick, except maybe old Glyffa; no one carried an extra load for him. He had watched some of his companions gorge themselves on inflated family shares of water, even Ebrahim. And still, the other boy, seeing half a literjon of brackish water untended, had drunk it, foolishly hoping no one would notice. How easy it had been for Ebrahim to blame it on his supposed friend when the theft was discovered. . . .

Upon driving Selim from the caves, Dhartha had refused to give him even a tiny water pouch for his journey, because that was considered a waste of tribal resources. None of them expected Selim to survive more than a day anyway, even if he somehow managed to avoid the fearsome monsters of the desert.

He muttered under his breath, knowing they couldn't hear him, "May your mouth fill with dust, Naib Dhartha." Selim bounded down the path away from the cliffs, while his people continued to utter curses from above. A hurled pebble bounced past him.

When he reached the base of the rock wall that stood as a shield against the desert and the sandworm demons, he set off in a straight line, wanting to get as far away as he could. Dry heat pounded on his head. Those watching him would surely be surprised to see him voluntarily hike out onto the dunes instead of huddling in a cave in the rocks.

What do I have to lose?

Selim made up his mind that he would never go back and plead for help. Instead, chin high, he strode across the dunes as far as he could. He would rather die than beg forgiveness from the likes of them. Ebrahim had lied to protect his own life, but Naib Dhartha had committed a far worse crime in Selim's eyes, knowingly condemning an innocent orphan boy to death because it simplified tribal politics.

Selim had excellent desert skills, but Arrakis was a severe environment. In the several generations since the Zensunni had settled here, no one had ever returned from exile. The deep desert swallowed them up, leaving no trace. He trudged out into the wasteland with only a rope slung over his shoulder, a stubby dagger at his belt, and a sharpened metal walking stick, a piece he had salvaged from the spaceport junkyard in Arrakis City.

Maybe Selim could go there and find a job with offworld traders, moving cargo from each vessel that landed, or stowing aboard one of the spaceships that plied their way from planet to planet, often taking years for each passage. But such ships only rarely visited Arrakis, since it was far from the regular shipping lanes. And joining the strange offworlders might make Selim give up too much of himself. It would be better to live alone in the desert—if he could survive. . . .

He pocketed another sharp rock, one that had been thrown from above. As the mountain buttress shrank into the distance, he found a third shard that seemed like a good throwing stone. Eventually, he would need to capture food. He could suck a lizard's moist flesh and live for just a little while longer.

As he made his way into the restless wasteland, Selim gazed toward a long peninsula of rock, far from the Zensunni caves. He'd be apart from the tribe there, but could still laugh at them every day he survived his exile. He could thumb his nose and call out jokes that Naib Dhartha would never hear.

Selim poked his walking stick into the soft dunes, as if stabbing an imaginary enemy. He sketched a deprecating Buddislamic symbol in the sand, with an arrow on it that pointed back toward the cliff dwellings. He took a special satisfaction from his defiance, even though the wind would erase the insult within a day. With a lighter step, he climbed a high dune and skidded down into the trough.

He began to sing a traditional song, maintaining an upbeat composure, and increased his speed. The distant peninsula of rock shimmered in the afternoon, and he tried to convince himself that it looked inviting. His bravado increased as he drew farther from his tormentors.

But when he was within a kilometer of the sheltering black rock, Selim felt the loose sand tremble under his feet. He looked up, suddenly realizing his danger, and saw ripples that marked the passage of a large creature deep beneath the dunes.

Selim ran. He slipped and scrambled across the soft ridge, desperate not to fall. He kept moving, racing along the crest, knowing that even this high dune would prove no obstacle for the oncoming sandworm. The rock peninsula remained impossibly far away, and the demon came ever closer.

Selim forced himself to skid to a halt, though his panicked heart urged him to keep running. Worms followed any vibration, and he had run like a terrified child instead of freezing in place like the wily desert hare. This behemoth had certainly targeted him by now. How many others before him had stood terrified, falling to their knees in final prayer before being devoured? No person had ever survived an encounter with one of the great desert monsters.

Unless he could fool it . . . distract it.

Selim willed his feet and legs to turn to stone. He took the first of the fist-sized stones he carried and hurled it as far as he could into the gully between dunes. It landed with a *thump*—and the ominous track of the approaching worm diverted just a little.

Selim tossed another rock, and a third, in a drumbeat pattern intended to lure the worm away from him. He threw the rest of his stones, and the beast turned only slightly, still rising up below him.

Empty handed, Selim now had no other way to divert the creature.

Its maw open wide, the worm gulped sand and stones, searching for a morsel of meat. The dune beneath Selim's boots shifted and crumbled, and he knew the monster would swallow him. He smelled an ominous cinnamon stench on the worm's breath, saw glimpses of fire in its gullet.

Naib Dhartha would no doubt laugh at the young

thief's fate. Selim shouted a loud curse. And rather than surrender, he decided to attack.

Closer to the cavernous mouth, the odor of spice intensified. The young man gripped his metal walking stick and whispered a prayer. As the worm lifted itself from beneath the dune, Selim leaped onto its curved and crusty back. He raised the metal staff like a spear and plunged the sharpened tip into what he thought would be tough, armored wormskin. Instead, the point slipped between segments, into soft pink flesh.

The beast reacted as if it had been shot with a hundred maula cannons. It reared up, thrashed and writhed.

Surprised, Selim drove the spear deeper and held on with all his strength. He squeezed his eyes shut, clenching his teeth and pulling back to keep himself steady. He would have no chance if he let go.

The little spear couldn't have wounded the demon; this was merely a human gesture of defiance, a biting fly thirsty for a sweet droplet of blood. Any moment now the worm would dive back beneath the sand and drag Selim down with it.

Surprisingly, though, the creature raced forward, keeping itself high out of the dunes where the exposed tissue would not be abraded by sand.

Terrified, Selim clung to the implanted staff—then laughed as he realized he was actually *riding* the monster! Shaitan himself! Had anyone ever done such a thing? If so, no man had ever lived to tell about it.

Selim made a pact with himself and with Buddallah that he would not be defeated, not by Naib Dhartha and not by this desert demon. He pulled back on his spear and pried the fleshy segment even wider, making the worm climb out of the sand, as if it could outrun the annoying parasite on its back. . . .

The young exile never made it to the strip of rock where he had hoped to establish a private camp. Instead, the worm careened into the deep desert . . . carrying Selim far from his former life.